A BLACK SWAN PROTECTION NOVELLA

Trust Me

HOPE SNYDER

TRUST ME

A BLACK SWAN PROTECTION NOVELLA

HOPE SNYDER

SUNNY LAUREL BOOKS

For Pondlife

CONTENTS

Chapter 1	1
Chapter 2	9
Chapter 3	18
Chapter 4	26
Chapter 5	33
Chapter 6	40
Chapter 7	48
Chapter 8	57
Chapter 9	68
Chapter 10	77
Chapter 11	86
Chapter 12	91
Chapter 13	98
Chapter 14	109
Chapter 15	115
Chapter 16	126
Chapter 17	132
Chapter 18	144
Chapter 19	150
Chapter 20	159
The Black Swan Protection Novellas	171
Acknowledgments	173
About the Author	175

CHAPTER 1

I TWIRL my red Montblanc pen between my fingers, then scribble the date on the pad of legal paper in front of me. The twentieth of February. The day everything fell apart and fell into place. Three years, seven months ago.

Looking up from the legal pad, I squint against the harsh winter sun shining through the windows of the conference room. It's catching Noa Ice's crystal-covered fingernails, causing them to flash rainbows at me as she repeatedly flips her blonde hair over her shoulder. She's leaning over the mahogany conference table, taking her time reading our terms and conditions, a teacup Yorkie tucked under her arm. Her financial counsel, Mr. Hartsher, sits to her right, murmuring answers to her questions. I'm unnerved by their delay.

Nearly four years on the job should mean I'm confident and comfortable as CEO of The Milenna Company, the world-renowned cosmetics and skincare conglomerate. I work endless hours, sleep minimally, focus all my brainpower on this job. But it's much more than a job, it's a legacy, a responsibility to do justice to our family name. I'm Laina Milenna, the last Milenna.

Mr. Delancey, Milenna's CFO, my right-hand advisor, and a de facto uncle, sits to my left. He's wearing a light gray suit that almost matches his silver hair. The rainbows from Noa's nails are making him look like a disco ball. He leans over to whisper to me as he tucks away his reading glasses, a recent acquiescence to his age. "I looked it over as we came in, they really don't have room to argue on this."

"Not at all," I murmur in agreement.

I check my watch, then the office bullpen outside the glass-walled conference room. My eye catches Dad's stern portrait on the far wall of the floor. His Mona Lisa smile and steely-eyed gaze is so sharp, I can almost hear him saying, *"Focus, Laina."* It's a handsome painting of him, depicting him as poised, sure, and calm.

At Mom and Dad's memorial service, Mr. Delancey gave the eulogy and I remember him saying, "Henry Milenna always had the right word at the right time, knew what to do in every situation, whose hand to shake, how to greet people in passing without being rude. He was suave and handsome and, well, just plain cool."

If Hollywood made a biopic of Dad, and I wouldn't be surprised if they did, I bet they'd cast someone epic like Tom Hardy as Henry Milenna. Dad is a lot to live up to, both in personality and in the running of the company.

"Ready for your vacation?" Mr. Delancey asks in a whisper. I smile and nod, feigning excitement. I'm not at all ready. So much could go wrong in just a few days, which is mostly why I haven't deviated from a pattern of tight control since I inherited this role. Taking a break for a week is a massive leap of faith and I'm anxious it won't be worth it.

I tuck my straight black hair behind my ear, determined to stay ahead of the worry mixed with sadness that presses on my heart. My mom's voice in my head soothes me with the same tone she would use when she'd make me yuja tea late at night, scooping the jam-like yuja-cheong into a mug and combining it with hot water.

We love you, Laina, no matter what.

The perfect balm for my insecurity.

A yip from Noa's Yorkie puppy startles me. Noa's now dabbing around her damp eyes with a tissue. She's three years older than me, a self-made millionaire thanks to social media, but an emerging disaster is making her brand an easy decision to acquire under our Beauty Done Well Initiative.

"We can't deny it's a generous offer, Miss Milenna," says Mr. Hartsher, breaking the standstill with his gravelly voice.

"It's more than generous, Mr. Hartsher," I reply. "You must realize the value of Nice Makeup is dropping by the minute. So far, we're tracking fifty beta testers posting to social media about how the makeup has burned their faces. This will only get worse before it gets better."

He clears his throat and leans over to sidebar with Noa as she stares daggers at me.

I glance away through the glass wall again and notice Everett, my executive protection agent, coming out of the elevator looking devastatingly handsome as always, one hand shoved in the pocket of his wool overcoat, the other holding what I know is an iced vanilla latte. It's winter in New York, but Everett knows I prefer my coffee cold in all seasons. He catches me watching him and swirls the coffee in my direction, earning a smile from me.

My assistant, Ainsley, greets him with a friendly, flirty, "Hey, Ev!" as he walks past her desk. Of course he doesn't ignore her, giving her a small wave and a smile, then leaning against an empty cubicle across from the conference room to wait for me.

His dark hair is pushed back off his forehead and gelled in place, showing off his structured face and always-aware brown eyes. He's the paragon of the chiseled bodyguard archetype from every Korean drama I used to watch, and I know I'm not the only one who thinks that.

A quick internet search for "Everett Park" reveals Pinterest boards, Reddit threads, and entire Instagram accounts dedicated to him. He's been with me since the day my parents died, and I've found him to be a walking paradox. He's all soft and thoughtful on the inside, powerful and intimidating on the outside.

I absolutely adore everything about him. But I keep that thought to myself at all times. I am his boss and we are both respectful, exemplary professionals.

"I don't get it," Noa cuts through my thoughts. Her dog echoes her with a bark.

"Which part, Miss Ice?" asks Mr. Delancey.

"Tell me again, Miss Laina Milenna, why you want to bail me out," Noa says, trying to stare me down. "I don't get what's in this for you if my brand is such a failure."

Heat rises in my cheeks and adrenaline jumps through me at her challenging tone.

"Your makeup is a nightmare for consumers and producers alike," I remind her. "This company and I have a personal mission to remove anything harmful from the beauty industry, including toxic beauty standards and harmful ingredients. And your brand has both. I feel—"

"Do you even know what it takes to get where I am today? How hard I've worked to launch this brand?" she shouts, her chin quivering. "You were born into this family, you inherited this job from good ol' Henry and Irene, you have had everything handed to you. You're a cosmetics billionaire by circumstance. I clawed my way through hell for this."

"My parents died!"

I can't believe she would call that having everything handed to me. Noa at least has the decency to look ashamed. My brain is screaming, *"How dare you say my parents' names like that?"*, but I have to stay composed. I do my best to speak in what I hope is a steady, threatening tone.

"You let a product with questionable ingredients onto the market, a product that has permanently scarred people. By allowing your launch to go forward, you have done nothing but insult your own credibility, as evidenced by the online laughingstock that you've become."

Noa has bigger tears falling faster now, but I have limited sympathy. You don't talk about my family that way. And if you're going to say you care about beauty products that will enhance people's lives, you don't release a product that you know is causing chemical burns. I want her products off the market and overseen by my labs that will ensure their quality going forward.

"It would be prudent to come to a decision now," I say. I glance at Mr. Delancey who gives me a nod of approval.

Mr. Hartsher dabs his forehead with a handkerchief, then once again leans over to Noa. She finally nods, and he clears his throat to speak. "Miss Milenna, Mr. Delancey, we agree to your terms."

I don't bother to hide my smile of triumph as I stand and extend my hand across the table. They both give me weak, dead-fish handshakes.

"Mr. Delancey will handle the paperwork and let you know what the next steps are. I look forward to our future meetings, Noa."

With that white lie, I collect my files off the table, shove them in my black Birkin bag, and grab my coat. I walk out the glass doors into the main bullpen of Milenna Headquarters, giving a mental salute to Dad's portrait.

Everett comes to my side immediately.

"You okay?" he asks, helping me into my camel coat.

"For now," I reply, as he hands me my coffee. I exhale with a curl of my lip and a bit of a growl. Noa Ice just made my unlikeable list.

Everett makes eye contact with me and the way he's pressing his lips together tells me he's concerned. It's the same look I get when I say that I'm staying late for the fourth night in a row. I collect those looks, wishing if I had enough, maybe someday I could trade them in for genuine care for me, Laina, not the CEO he's hired to protect.

I give him a short nod and tilt my head towards Ainsley's desk, where she's waiting for me to come over and do our daily debrief.

"There's nothing left for you to do except vacation! Have fun!" Ainsley exclaims with a little squeal and jazz hands as we approach. She's always a ray of sunshine, a stark contrast to the sharp, curt assistants I've run across in the gray world of corporate business.

"Thanks, Ains," I say with a smile. "See you soon."

We give each other a quick hug and she whispers, "Don't worry about a thing."

That feels completely outside the realm of possibility.

Everett gets the elevator for us and I'm about to step inside when I hear Mr. Delancey shout my name. I turn to see him jogging across the floor towards us.

"I'll hold the elevator," says Everett, patient as always.

I hurry to meet Mr. Delancey the last few paces.

"I almost forgot, one last thing, I promise, then I'll wish you 'Bon Voyage'," Mr. Delancey says, slightly breathless. "You know Lourden Luxuries? Adam Lourden's company?"

"Yeah, of course." I know the company in the business sense, but my mind also flashes back to the day their family made headlines. To the day my parents sat huddled on the couch in the living room, crying in each other's arms. When I asked what was wrong, Dad pointed to a newspaper lying on the coffee table with the headline, "Lourden Luxuries CEO and Wife Killed in Crash off Williamsburg Bridge." My parents were mourning like they'd just lost old friends, but I had never heard the name before then. I shake my head to clear the memory as I tune back to what Mr. Delancey's saying.

"They want to develop an upscale skincare or perfume line with us."

Lourden Luxuries is a dynasty as big as The Milenna Company. They operate as a broker, dealer, and facilitator for exchanges of luxury goods: art, cars, collectibles, wine, etc. It's not outside the scope of their company to want to try their hand at something like this and I'm actually surprised it hasn't happened sooner.

"How do you feel about it?" asks Mr. Delancey.

"Neutral. Maybe next fall, do a special release for the holidays?"

He nods and writes a note on his iPad. "I'll let them know. Okay, that's all, I promise. Bon Voyage, Laina."

I'm about to ask him a quick follow-up question that's been plaguing me about my standing with the board at the moment, but as if reading my mind, he pats my shoulder. "Stop trying to find things to worry about."

"If you say so," I mumble with a begrudging smile. I wave to him and finally join Everett in the elevator.

CHAPTER 2

ONCE THE SILVER doors roll closed on us, I let out a huge sigh that ends in a surprising, hiccup-like sob.

"I heard what that girl said in the conference room," Everett says, the deep bass of his voice calming and reassuring me. "That was low."

I wish we had the kind of relationship where I could turn towards him and curl up in his arms, or at least lean against his stalwart shoulder for comfort. Instead, I back up and slump against the wall to his left, closing my eyes.

I need a second, just one moment to collect myself. All the outward armor I don to be a tough, shrewd twenty-six-year-old CEO is powerless against someone saying my parents' names out loud.

"It's good you're going on vacation," Everett says.

I nod and allow myself to verbalize the truth. "I'm tired." Saying it out loud is like letting a huge boulder roll off my back, but it also feels like admitting defeat.

"You are so tired, Laina," he replies, sounding relieved to be able to say it.

I glance at him in surprise and wait for him to look me in the eye, but he keeps his gaze straight ahead. He's usually so hesitant to confront me. Even when I fell asleep in my tray of sushi on top of all my notes for the annual shareholders' meeting, he didn't say I should have gone home sooner or called it quits or taken better care of myself. To hear him make an observation about me that's remotely negative is new territory. And a little thrilling.

"What about you, are you tired?" I ask, pressing back.

He's seen me every single day, including every holiday, every weekend—he's never taken time off. He's the only one who sees me cry, he's seen me angry, seen me celebrate my biggest wins with silly happy dances in the car. He's helped with wardrobe malfunctions, even carried tampons in his jacket pocket. So, isn't he tired too?

But he doesn't answer and I don't ask again. Every so often, I brush up against firm boundaries that Everett has in place. Discussing his personal state of wellness is one of those. I switch to a breezier topic. "What are you going to do while I'm gone?"

"Read, sleep in. I have some research I've been assigned by the home office at Black Swan Protection."

I'm surprised his agency gave him homework, especially on his first break in years. "Researching what?"

"The Vidovic Group."

"The Vidovic Group? What's that?"

"A criminal organization out of Eastern Europe. Pretty nefarious: drug runners, human traffickers, they run a big weapons black market. They've paid off most justice systems to turn a blind eye to them."

"We're going to have the most opposite weeks possible," I say with a laugh.

He grins at me and there's no quelling the butterflies in my stomach. His grin is my favorite for how genuine it is, wide and unabashed. I can't help but smile back as we stride across the lobby and out the doors into the cold sunshine.

The buzz of reporters and instant shouts fill the air. Multiple camera shutters burst into action. A quick scan of the area tells me it's a bigger day than normal for the paparazzi. They must be waiting for the gorgeous, disgraced Noa Ice.

On my left, a guy in a hoodie and baseball cap stands with his hands shoved in his pockets. What's a paparazzo doing without a recording device or a camera? I watch him, he watches me watching him, and a chill goes down my spine. My hand involuntarily grabs Everett's arm. He looks down at me, catching my expression, then stands tall, going on high alert.

"On our left" I say in a low voice. "Texas Rangers hat, no camera."

Everett switches to walk on my left side.

Ever since the untimely death of my parents, I've had an irrational fear that there's some sort of Milenna curse, that I might be the next one taken too soon. Watching this strange guy, the fear pops up again, like an ugly jack-in-the-box. My body goes into fight or flight mode.

The guy suddenly whips his right arm out of his pocket and I flinch, shying into Everett.

"It's okay, I'm here. It's just a phone." Everett puts his arm around my shoulders as we keep walking towards the car. He's almost tripping me as he pushes us forward while keeping an eye on the sketchy guy who's holding up a cell phone. He opens the passenger door and stands over me as I get in, immediately closing the door behind me.

Everett slides into the driver's seat and guns the car into an opening in traffic. He keeps pivoting to look out the window and behind us and it's not until we're through an intersection that he sits back in his seat and says, "Probably nothing. Good eye though."

My hands are shaking and I reach for my purse to channel my frayed nerves by searching for my phone. I hate this overwhelming feeling of vulnerability. I'm the one in control, I'm the one in power, but why is it that those at the top are usually targeted?

After shuffling things around for a moment, I shut my bag in frustration.

"Should I be going on vacation alone?" I ask out loud.

"It was you and Tara's idea to go alone," Everett says. "I initially advised against it."

My one concession to needing outside help in my life is my therapist, Tara. After a massive panic attack and worrisome cardiac symptoms landed me in the hospital a few months ago, I asked if I could just take some anti-anxiety medication and get back to work.

Instead, Tara and my doctor prescribed a vacation. As in travel for fun, travel without any business meetings. Relax. They said if I didn't take a break, I'd just start a downward spiral that would lead to serious, irreversible health problems. I rolled my eyes, but after Ainsley, Mr. Delancey, and Everett conspired together and badgered me for weeks on end, I gave in. "Purely for a change of scenery," was the reason I gave.

While going alone was ultimately my decision, there was also a bit of reverse psychology involved. Tara kept sending me articles about "travel therapy," then articles about solo travel, then loads of articles about group wellness retreats. The only thing worse than traveling alone is traveling with strangers, so I overreacted and picked solo travel. Then I panicked further, closed my eyes, pointed to a map, and picked the Maldives as my destination. Making travel plans in a state of anxiety is not the best course of action.

Everett glances over at me.

"You will be totally fine, Laina," he says. "I would say no outright if it wasn't going to be okay."

I lean my head in my hand against the car window. "I'm going to miss you though," I say. Friends say that. It's not too forward.

Everett gives me a soft, half grin. "It's good you're going, you need some space from all of us. Be lonely, it'll help you."

Be lonely? That sounds awful. I'm used to the constant, consistent presence of Ainsley and Mr. Delancey at the office and Everett, well, everywhere. For almost four years.

I take a deep breath and catch a whiff of roses. *Three years, seven months.* Oh no.

"Did I just almost forget?" I ask out loud, sitting upright.

"I wouldn't let you," says Everett. Now I notice we're following a familiar route through the city and it's not towards the airport. I check the back seat and sure enough, there are two bouquets of deep crimson roses with wide black ribbon tied around the stems.

"Thank you," I say, moved that Everett remembered this for me. "Thank you so much. You are so thoughtful."

"Of course," he murmurs back, like it's no big deal. But it is to me. My heart squeezes with emotion.

When we pull into the cemetery, I'm swimming in

shame that I nearly left on vacation, forgetting it was the monthly anniversary of my parents' passing, forgetting to come see them. It hits me in a weird part of my heart. Will I do this forever? But I never want to stop coming back to this touchpoint. It's a reminder of how and why I am what I am.

Everett parks the car, does a quick scan of our surroundings, then comes around to my side and opens the door for me. He gets the roses out of the back seat and eases them into my waiting arms.

I walk up the small grassy hill alone, stepping on the pavers to avoid my heels sinking down. Standing in front of their side-by-side stones, I exhale, soft and weak. The previous bouquets have been cleared away and the names, "Henry Conrad Ernest Milenna" and "Irene Louise Lee Milenna," carved into the marble are stark and sharp. I close my eyes to picture them.

Mom: beautiful, elegant, loving.

Dad: smart, shrewd, charismatic.

I picture the day before they left, all of us congregating in the kitchen. Dad making us laugh with a joke he heard in a board meeting. Mom casually kneading bread dough like a modern-day pioneer. Them kissing in passing. It was idyllic. It was perfection. It was a dream.

I am what's left of that.

The routine of my visit clicks into place: set down the roses, run my fingers over their inscriptions, press a kiss to each of their names.

I sniffle and shove my fists in my coat pockets, finding something crinkly and plastic in my right pocket—a pack of tissues that wasn't there this morning. I glance over my shoulder at Everett, slowly pivoting from left to right, watching over me. He really does think of everything.

I wipe my nose, dab at my eyes. Okay, this is it. Time to leave. Time to go. The worst part is walking away, but I manage because what other option is there?

We drive to the airfield in silence. Everett parks next to my private jet and I muster my best "all is fine" bravado as I get out, gathering my coat around me.

"Take care of this for me," I say, passing my phone to Everett. I promised to completely disconnect while on this trip, but leaving my phone is like cutting the anchor of routine off my boat of sanity.

He tucks my phone into the breast pocket of his suit jacket. "Take care of yourself. Rest well."

I put my hand on his arm, hoping I can siphon some strength from his solid biceps.

"You too, Ev."

I hazard a glance at his eyes as the pilot starts warming up the engines. I'm walking onto the plane without my bodyguard, going somewhere without my shadow, and it's no easy feat.

Everett looks on the verge of saying something, but instead he takes a small step forward and puts his hands on my shoulders. Warmth runs through my coat, down my arms, reassuring me. I cup my hands around his arms, just above his elbows. Are we hugging? Is this a hug for us?

As I'm about to step back, he looks down at me at the last moment. There's something different in his eyes, something vulnerable. Butterflies take flight in my stomach. I've never had to say goodbye to him before, not like this. I don't know what to do or say.

"I should go," I say and with a quick smile, I turn away.

I've taken three steps towards the plane when I hear, "Laina, wait."

I whip around to find Everett with his hands shoved in his coat pockets, his overcoat blowing in the wind, studying the tops of his black dress shoes.

"Come here," he says. He looks nervous and worried and it's making me nervous on his behalf. I cross back to him, coming closer so I have a chance of hearing him.

"What is it?" I ask.

"I didn't want to tell you before you left, but now I feel like I have to."

"Are you okay?" I ask, immediately fearing the worst. If he says he has a terminal disease, I'm going to collapse right here on the tarmac. If he needs a kidney or bone marrow or half a liver, I'm going to be the first on the list to be tested for compatibility.

"My contract is up in a few weeks."

Thank goodness. Business. I can do business.

"Oh. I didn't realize that," I reply. "Do we need to renegotiate terms? I mean, you definitely deserve a raise, you're one of the most essential people in my life."

Everett presses a hand over his eyes and takes a shaky breath. He shakes his head, as if the answers to all my questions about him are "No." When he clears his throat and looks out over my head, he seems distant, far away from this moment.

"I've requested a reassignment and Black Swan Protection has informed me it will be an international posting. You'll be notified of your new security detail before I leave."

My mouth drops open. He may as well have punched me

in the stomach. I'm speechless and frozen in place. I don't know if I want to cry or get angry.

"Why?" I manage to breathe out, my voice shaking with disappointment, sadness, shock.

Everett stands tall, shoves his hands in his coat, and puts on a mask of disinterest.

"It's what's best for me and my career."

It's a slap across the face. Three and a half years together, living in the same house, going to the same places, doing everything together, without a hint that he would ever leave.

He's moving on. For his career.

"Everett...." I don't know how to finish my sentence. It takes me a minute to find my words again. "You've been the most fantastic bodyguard. You'll still be here when I get back?"

He smiles, but there's a hint of scoffing as he nods back. There's something especially wrong with this entire conversation. I wish I had the time to sit here and figure it out, but someone near the plane yells out it's time to leave.

"You should go," says Everett. He steps back, leaving me exposed to the cold wind rushing across the tarmac. "It'll be okay," he adds with a nod.

"Okay, see you later," I say in a rush and I speed walk to the stairs.

I think I hear him say, "Be safe, Laina," but it's lost in the whirring engines.

CHAPTER 3

THE FLIGHT IS LONG, and there are a few extra legs of travel to get to the resort that I'm staying at. By the time I let myself into my private villa, I've been awake for more hours than I care to count. When I finally flop onto the crisp white sheets covering the king-sized hotel bed, I fall asleep to the faint smell of seawater and the sound of gentle waves.

My first full day in the Maldives mostly consists of fidgeting. Without the usual distractions of my laptop and folders and phone, I'm at a loss for how to fill my time. I swim, order room service, scan the TV channels, find nothing that grips me. My mind just isn't in relaxation mode, as evidenced by the hotel notepad covered in notes for our next board meeting.

On the second day, I walk around the hotel grounds a little, kill ninety minutes with a massage, and swim some more. The ocean is mostly empty, except for a little white boat that belongs to the resort running a few errands back and forth past my particular cluster of villas. As I dive into the clear water again, my therapist's one assignment for my trip starts to creep into my mind.

I can hear Tara's soothing, zen voice in my head. "I want you to write, Laina. For at least three of your vacation days, I want you to get a journal, open up a blank page, and try to unpack the past few years. You've been in survival mode for so long, I doubt you've processed things well. Let all your emotions come to the surface. Follow whatever comes to mind and write it all down."

No thanks.

I head to the central resort area for a grueling round of hot yoga, but eventually I reach the end of my distractions. I don't break out my journal just yet, but I take a long walk towards yet another beach and decide to mentally rehash something not quite as delicate as my family—my love life. It's not my main assignment, but it's what comes to mind. Especially with the thought of Everett's imminent departure.

I've done my best to not think about his announcement at all and the resort is so secluded, safety hasn't been a concern. I step off the boardwalk and onto the beach, turn in a little circle to take in the sharp contrast of the golden sand and blue water, a line of palm trees behind the sand.

A shadow shifts behind one of them and I do a double-take. But it's just a bird rustling, then flying away. My feet take me to the water's edge and I twist my hair in one hand to keep it from floating across my face in the breeze.

Right, my love life.

My last significant relationship feels like ages ago, a big, splashy to-do while I was still in college. On a family trip to Europe, I happened to meet a hot, up-and-coming Formula 1 driver and fell madly in lust with him. We were obsessed with each other and the media was obsessed with us. I traveled to all his races, and he won the world championship two years in a row, the two years we were together.

Our fiery interest eventually waned and we broke up, a mutual decision. But then, coincidentally or not, he never won again. My name and the word "curse" made a lot of headlines and fans were livid, the paparazzi incessant. I had a bodyguard for that season, but it was some older guy that was nowhere near as interesting or attractive as Everett.

I had a very quick rebound with an actor who shot to popularity after playing the male lead in a popular Nicholas Sparks movie. I realized too late he really only needed a girlfriend for awards season. He dumped me as soon as the last after-party was over.

Up until that point, I was young and a sucker for a whirlwind romance. But after that burn, I resolved to wait around for something serious, true love with a soulmate. When my parents died, my life filled so quickly with urgent, immediate needs, all my own dreams got sucked away, including love. It was like falling into a black hole, the black hole of The Milenna Company.

Love is a word that is not in my vocabulary these days.

When day four dawns, I groan and huff and roll my eyes thinking about the assignment. I can't put it off much longer. After breakfast, I drag myself to my near-empty suitcase, pull out the journal I packed, take a pen from the desk, and sit on a chaise lounge overlooking the lagoon. With one last eye twitch of reluctance, I write.

"I always wanted to be a CEO of my own company. I was ready to rise to the challenge of being just like Dad, albeit on a smaller scale. Henry Milenna, revered, universally acknowledged as a titan of the industry, magnetic and smart. I followed

the golden path that would ensure I could do the same thing with my own brand, under the Milenna umbrella. I pushed myself to finish college in three years, tacked on a rigorous MBA in twelve months, started to formulate my goals and products for my own cosmetics line. But then the plane crashed. When we reviewed the legal documents afterwards, we discovered Dad had preserved the CEO role at The Milenna Company for me."

I set the pen and journal down on the deck and drop my head in my hands with a groan. I may be number one on the "30 under 30" lists and my name crops up on round-ups like "North America's Most Famous CEOs," but deep down I'm just a kid that wants to make her parents proud, to do well with what they've left me, their last request.

"Is this how it's going to be forever? Or does there come a point where my own dreams are going to matter again? I can't live in their shadow forever."

Mom was the queen of New York society. She ran the amazing Irene Milenna Opera Foundation, and hosted tons of charity functions, all while maintaining her genuine love for others. She was never fake about helping people. She was devoted to and hopelessly in love with Dad. And because she was the same person inside the doors of our historic brownstone as she was out in the echelons of the rich and famous, I trusted her, emulated her, and wanted nothing more than to be as graceful of a woman as she was.

But I mostly wanted my life to look like Dad's. A powerful business magnate, brave, willing to do gutsy things that always pay off. Since filling his shoes, I've made some big moves, the biggest being my Beauty Done Well Initiative, but even that was fraught with insecurity on my part.

I wish I could have something for myself, a role that I can

have full confidence in, that can accommodate me having a life and balance outside of work. Dad seemed to have that, why is it so elusive for me?

I unearth a deeper question, the one that keeps me up at night. "*If Dad walked into The Milenna Company today, would he be proud of me?*"

———

THE BAR in the main building of the hotel is an open-air arrangement of wicker furniture and giant palm fans overhead, wafting sea air throughout the veranda. I find a seat in the shade and order a Mai Tai. Other than the ambient music, there's a natural silence on the island that is supposed to be soothing, but I'm struggling to adjust to it after living my entire life in the noise of the city.

Without a screen in front of me, I'm free to admire the way the sunset colors of my drink meld together in the tall glass, but it quickly gives way to worry about our stock graphs. There's no hum of conversation, no buzz of phones, nothing to remind me of Milenna. I miss Ainsley's chatter and Everett's eyes and Mr. Delancey's questions. I miss their constancy, our inside jokes, knowing I'm going to see them every day and we'll pick up with the same sentence we left off on.

A bachelorette party settles in a few couches over from me, a bunch of bubbly girls, cheering and toasting over and over again. I almost look to the side to exchange an eye roll with Everett. But I stop just before I embarrass myself. He's not here and I can't hear his occasional, casual laugh for a few more days.

And then only a couple more weeks until I lose it forever.

It's not like he's going to keep in touch with me. I have to be honest with myself. Ainsley jokes that we're work husband and wife, which always gives me a little thrill, but once that work is over, we're just two people who probably would never naturally cross paths.

The girls next to me explode with laughter and I have to admit, as loud as they are, they look like they're having fun. The one in a white sundress and a tiara must be the bride. I don't know if this kind of bachelorette fling is what I would want, but I do envy her happiness, the jokes about her groom to be, the blush on her cheeks.

Well, if that's what I want, I should start dating again. There's a part of me that would love nothing more than to have a partner, a spouse, another person to help balance me out. But the word "dating" screams of wasted time, stilted conversations, incompatibility smacking me in the face over and over.

If only there was a handsome, caring man already in my life that I may or may not already have a massive crush on and may or may not have had a steamy dream about kissing in a crowded bar.

No, no, I can't go down that road. Everett is my friend who has never been anything but professional and caring towards me. He's never given me the slightest hint of interest.

We make pointed efforts to stay far away from anything that would give any mixed signals. Because of how relatively close in age we are, how attractive Everett is, and how buzzy my name can be, there are always rumors circling and attempts to make us more than we are.

The worst was the first time the media really saw us

together, the day of my parents' memorial service. Everett had put his hand on my back at some point as we came down the cathedral stairs and the cameras went wild. The picture was all over the tabloids and of course I looked sick and distraught and he looked cool yet comforting.

After that I learned how much of a spin they could really put on the two of us. It still comes up from time to time, but we both make an effort to make it a non-issue.

Even outside of the public eye, Everett and I have never crossed any lines. I wish I could tell him how I feel, especially now that he's leaving, but I would be risking way too much if I let myself test the waters only to be politely rebuffed. That would officially be the death of "us," and our friendship is too important. I wouldn't want to ruin it right at the end and tarnish our entire history together.

I tip the bartender and make my way towards the beach to wander along the water for a bit. The cerulean waves are so clear I almost don't want to stir up the creamy sand with my footsteps. I slip my sandals off and swear I'll only think happy, positive thoughts, do a review of my highlights.

Like how I acquired Nice Makeup, taking yet another toxic makeup company off the market. How my Beauty Done Well Initiative is gaining traction in the cosmetics world. I'm excited to see my name and position being used to influence things for the better. Tara might kindly hint with indirect phrases that my personal life is crap, but my professional life is moving forward in a positive direction.

A staff member walks towards me, a stack of towels balanced on one hand. He's wearing a white panama hat and sunglasses, but I can see a significant burn on the left side of his face. As he comes near, I prepare a smile of acknowledgement. But instead of walking past me with a nod, he slows down and stops in front of me.

"Can I walk with you, Laina?" he asks.

His voice is low, raspy, and *familiar,* making my heart stop and my knees shake. I look at the man's face, searching to find anything recognizable behind the taut, twisting burn on his face. I try to pick out an arching gray eyebrow or straight-lipped mouth, but whatever marred his appearance has done significant damage. There's nothing about this man that I know, but he knows my name. And that voice.

He takes off his sunglasses and with one quick glance from his grey-blue eyes, I'm a daughter again, being put in my place with a stern look.

"Dad?" I ask, wavering and weak. "You're alive?"

CHAPTER 4

"DON'T HUG ME, don't react, just keep walking down the beach," Dad says. Is this a hallucination? Did someone put something in my Mai Tai?

Dad's hand presses against my back, propelling me into my first step. This is real. As we walk, I check over my shoulder to make sure there are two sets of footprints in the sand. There are.

"What is going on?" I splutter in disbelief and shock. "It's...it's been four years."

"You've grown up," he says, looking me over without meeting my eyes. "You've done well for yourself. I'm impressed."

I study Dad's face, trying to understand.

"You're a dead man. I put flowers on your grave. They said there wasn't even anything left of you to put in the—"

There wasn't anything left of him to put in the casket.

Because he wasn't dead.

Dad waves his hand in front of us like none of that matters. "I don't have much time and I need your help with something." He sets the towels down on a nearby chair and keeps walking. He won't look me in the eye. This is not the Dad I lost.

I stop in place, forcing him to react. He shoots me a piercing gaze and, there, that's Dad's glare. I nod to indicate that somehow I'm processing and listening, and resume walking. My eyes choose to fixate on the foamy edge of the water to keep from breaking down and weeping.

"The plane crash was a hijacking," Dad says. "It was ordered by a powerful enemy I made long before you were born. He's the reason your mother is dead. I somehow walked away from the crash, away from her broken body."

His words conjure a horrifying image and oxygen is in short supply as I shudder.

"Deep breaths, Laina. There's more."

"How did you know where I was?" I ask, brushing tears off my cheeks.

"I've been keeping tabs on you. I have some friends in the cyber realm who helped me arrange this."

"You, what, you're like living off the grid, hiding out in the dark web or something?" He shakes his head like that's a stupid question and maybe it is. "So why was the plane hijacked?"

"I used to be best friends with Vanya Vidovic."

My jaw drops and my limbs go numb.

"Vanya Vidovic? As in the Vidovic Group?" As in the criminal group Everett is currently researching.

Dad nods with a wry laugh as he urges me to keep walking. "See, you've heard of them. Vanya and I went all through boarding school, then college together. When we were juniors in college, he inherited his father's extensive crime organization in Eastern Europe. I tried to talk him out of going down that path, tried to get him to stay in the U.S., but the pressure to uphold his family legacy was too great. When he left for Albania, I cut ties with him."

"Why would he come for you then?" I ask.

"There was another friend that went through school with Vanya and I, the third member of our trio—Adam Lourden. Recognize that name?"

"Lourden Luxuries," I murmur in disbelief. "The Lourden car crash."

"Adam worshiped Vanya and ended up laundering money for him, until his guilty conscience pricked at him shortly after. But at that point he couldn't get out. So, he decided to be a mole, feeding evidence to me. He trusted me to hold it for him and together we worked to form a dossier to turn over to law enforcement."

I know where this is going now. "But Vanya found out and had him killed."

Dad nods. "I thought I would be in the clear, that he wouldn't come for our family. But that was false hope. I haven't returned to you, to the city, to Milenna because it's too dangerous and I need to finish this once and for all."

My pulse is picking up and adrenaline is surging through me. I'm barely keeping up, but I'm hanging on to what Dad's insinuated. He can't come back until the threat is gone.

"So, we could be a family again," I say. "Once Vanya Vidovic is arrested."

"For that to happen, there's something I need you to do," he responds. "I need you to access the dossier and covertly get it to my associate. Once I have the evidence and we file the case with a few, select justice departments, we'll be in the clear. Vanya must be stopped, nothing else matters."

He's saying this like it's as easy as buying a cup of coffee on the way to work. Like I'm some experienced secret spy and this is something I can simply do during a lunch break.

"You are the only one who can help me with this, Laina," he says. "I can't risk going back to the house, back to the city. I have to stay a dead man. But you've never made a move against the Vidovic Group. For three years you've been silent, you'll be flying under the radar. You have a bodyguard too, right?"

I nod as I press my fingers to my temples. I can't believe Everett's not here for this. Dad comes around to stand in front of me, finally looking me in the eye with conviction.

"The Vidovic Group is an unchecked menace that must be stopped. I have to defeat them, ruin Vanya. I've done everything I can on my own to collect more evidence, but the last piece of the puzzle, the final nail in the coffin is the evidence in the dossier. Get it for me and all will be made right."

I meet his gaze and wonder why his fatherly instincts don't seem to sense the fear rolling off me. There's no comfort coming from him. If it were Mom, she'd be hugging me breathless.

Dad doesn't say a thing, just rests his hand on my shoulder, looking at me with expectation, his hand feeling heavier by the second. I fill in the words for him. He needs me to do this, I can make him proud if I do this, I can do this for him, for Mom, for our family to be together again.

"What do I have to do?" I ask, straightening my back and squaring my shoulders.

"Do you still have the family safe?"

I nod. "It's in my closet now."

"Good. When you open it, use your handprint like you normally do, but punch in your social security number before opening it. There's a false bottom. Access that and wait for further instructions. If anyone asks for a passphrase, tell them 'It's snowing in the Black Hills.' Got it?"

I nod, repeating it to myself under my breath. He starts to back away from me and I strain to activate all my senses, to trap the feeling of his presence.

"Remember, you cannot tell anyone that I'm alive," he says. "Keep yourself safe by keeping this secret."

"Can I tell Mr. Delancey?"

"No. No one. If something were to happen, I need you to deny my existence."

"I'll perjure myself if I have to."

Dad smiles and I take a mental snapshot of him; a lopsided smile, a creased face, but still those cutting steel eyes.

"That'll be the day," he says. "My rule-follower child perjuring herself."

"I want us to be a family again, if we can."

"Of course, I know you want that," Dad says.

"Will I see you again here?" I ask.

"No, I'll leave the Maldives immediately."

I nod and my body struggles between crying, clinging, or composing myself. I go with the latter.

"Dad—"

"Laina, make me proud."

I reach for him with open arms, the way I used to when I was a little kid. My need to hug him is desperate. He sighs, like he's about to deny me, so I lunge for him, wrapping my arms around him. We give each other a hug so brief, I barely get to close my eyes and absorb it. I've longed for this for years and it's too short, too painful. Dad kisses my forehead and walks away without another word.

I stumble to reach my villa. When the door clicks closed behind me, my face contorts with emotion and tears cloud my eyes. I murmur his instructions over and over and over, giving them their own rhythm. "Family safe, social security number, false bottom, wait for instructions, 'It's snowing in the Black Hills'."

My dad is alive, but I'm so confused. If I had allowed myself to imagine a reunion with my parents, in my wildest dreams, it would have had tearful hugs, laughs of disbelief, so many kisses and hands on cheeks, absorbing the presence of each other. Dad was almost in another world, one where I barely exist. But he's alive. He's alive.

I collapse on the bed and my mind whirls until I fall asleep hours later, alone in the dark.

THE NEXT TWO days turn into the opposite of what this trip was intended to be. Instead of relaxing and journaling and swimming with dolphins, I stay in my room and obsessively think over the present, the past, the future.

My dad turning out to be alive is a domino falling, with massive implications. Once I get this done, his enemies are arrested, put behind bars, ended. Then Henry Milenna comes back to the world, I'll step down from CEO, he resumes his rightful role, everything flips again. I'll be free to pursue my own wants and dreams, things will be so different.

That's the future, but in the present, I still have to get this done. Who is going to be coming after me? Will I know danger before I see it? My sleep is filled with nightmares of running and falling in a black hole, planes dropping out of the sky, files with papers spilling everywhere. Everything grows heavier as questions plague me.

The hotel computer gets a lot of use from me as I do cursory research on the Vidovic Group. Simple scans of news articles bring to life just how atrocious this group is, especially its leader, Vanya Vidovic. A real villain's villain.

I need to get home, to get the ball rolling on this mission. I can't be here any more. I quickly call up my plane to be ready to leave in a few hours and send an email from the hotel computer to Everett that I'm coming back. It's cutting my vacation short, but the secret is weighing on me like a boulder in a backpack that I can't take off.

The whole flight back I think about the new direction my life is taking. Dad's given me a straightforward task with maximum reward at the end: a reunion and a step back. I'm overwhelmed with the urge to metaphorically tidy up the company and make sure everything is ship-shape for his eventual return. There's a new purpose, a new focus for now. Dad's going to make a comeback, I'm going to be more free, it's going to be amazing. Just a little bit of pressure, then it'll be over.

CHAPTER 5

As I come down the steps of the plane, I'm greeted with the sight of Everett leaning against the town car, looking stunning without trying, pressing his tie to his chest to keep it from fluttering in the wind.

Exactly the person I wanted to see. Strong, steady, stalwart. Leaving soon. Comforting and unnerving at the same time. But then he starts pacing, shoulders tight.

"Hey," I say as I get closer. "What's wrong?"

He holds up his hand to stop my next word. He points to the car. I raise an eyebrow, then shake my head. I don't understand.

"Listen to me," he says, stepping away from the car and into my space. His voice is stern and low, and he leans in close enough to be heard over the jet engines winding down. "Don't say anything about anything until we get home and I say it's okay."

"What?" I reel back from him.

"Don't say anything on the drive home. I still have your phone and it's off, so no one else knows you're home yet."

Warning bells are going off in my head.

"Ev, what's going on? You think the car is bugged or something?"

He nods. "Do you trust me?"

Who do I trust? This news about Dad has a million repercussions and there's an element of danger surrounding it. If I let Everett in on this and he leaks it to his protection agency, I'm unsure whether that's a good or a bad thing. His agency has a global presence, and he said they're looking into the Vidovic Group. It would be a relief to share this weighty secret with someone. I want to sleep without fear.

I look up into Everett's dark eyes. Knowing that he has been nothing but loyal and protective of me, I find it hard to suspect him of betraying my confidence. His gaze is pleading, entreating, tugging on my heart.

"I trust you."

He nods, relieved. "I'll explain everything as soon as I can."

As promised, it's a quiet drive home. I stare out the window at the blur of the city and feel like I'm in a snow globe, reeling from having everything turned upside down one too many times. Fear is rising, but I tamp it down. I only fear two things—paper cuts and snakes.

"What are you afraid of?" I suddenly ask Everett. "Do you have a phobia?"

"Knives."

I smile. "You're a bodyguard afraid of knives?"

"They're not correlated. It's not like I chose it from a line-up."

"True. What would you have chosen, if you could?"

"Bears. Or sharks. If I stick to working in large cities, I'll never have to encounter them."

"But you have to use knives to cook. I've seen you chop stuff."

"I've trained myself to conquer my weakness," he says, ever so serious, but with a glint of humor in his eyes. I chuckle and shake my head. Should have known he'd have a well-thought-out answer.

When we get back to the house, we go through our usual routine of me taking off my coat and hanging it on the coat rack by the back door while Everett loosens his tie and takes his jacket off.

But as I turn to walk to my room and change out of my traveling clothes, Everett gently grabs my elbow. I freeze. He runs his hand down my arm to catch my fingers, a deep warmth trailing his touch. It's sudden and unexpected and I wouldn't be surprised to find the sleeve of my silk blouse incinerated. He has never touched me so intimately and it's making me far too hopeful.

"Laina," he says in a husky voice.

My stomach flips. That was not a touch of protection and that voice, that tone, it's not one of warning or caution. I look up at him and the intensity in his eyes is new. I'm desperate to know what's going through his mind right now.

"I'm going to say something and all I need is a yes or no answer." He swallows and it's loud in the pensive silence. "I'm doing this because I care about you and you are my responsibility. I am still your bodyguard and I am not going to leave you on your own."

He's taking his time to clarify that this is just a job for him. But ridiculous hope still flares in my chest.

"If you want to tell me about what happened on your trip," he says in a voice that is dropping closer and closer to a whisper, "in order for both of us to be protected, you have to... we need to get married."

I blink.

"You want to marry me?" I ask, slow and deliberate, not wanting any miscommunication on this point.

He nods. "Yes."

Be still, my heart.

"If we are married, the law considers us one," he clarifies. "Whatever we say to each other is protected and we cannot be called to testify against each other. Whatever we talk about is completely confidential, a secret between the two of us."

My eyes go wide and I'm trying to remind myself to breathe. He's thought about this already. Wait, he knows something. There's something going on. And I don't miss the way that this isn't about want for him. This is a need. Not for love, but for legal reasons, and his job as my bodyguard.

I put my hand out to steady myself and end up grabbing his forearm. This proposal is the strangest, most brilliant solution I could have possibly come up with. But holy crap.

I avoid meeting his gaze, not wanting him to see how much this is affecting me. I realize he's only proposing a marriage of convenience, legal convenience, but there's danger in this too. I would be in grave danger of loving and losing him in a way that would break me.

Everett takes my hands and I grasp onto his like a drowning person. He clears his throat. "I don't know where the line is, if this is totally unprofessional," he says. "But I want to help you. And whatever may be going on, I need to know it all in order to protect you well."

I allow myself to look in his eyes. His face is earnest and reassuring, not a trace of ulterior motives. I take a deep breath and slowly let it out. I need him. I trust him. And there's a part of me that desperately wants to lean into the make-believe, the fairytale, and allow myself this one last daydream come to life —marrying Everett.

"Why are you doing this? You're leaving in a few weeks," I remind him.

"And I'll do my job well here, right up until the minute I leave you," he says with promise in his eyes. I hate hearing him use the word "leave," but I love his eyes. I love his loyalty and his caring heart. I love everything about him. As a friend, of course. I can allow myself to say I love him without it meaning something with real feelings. I can admire and adore him without falling for him.

I can do professional. I can. This is nothing different than another day on the job for both of us. Working and living with Everett is like constantly walking past a statue in a fine art museum. I can admire its exquisiteness, the handsome details and distinguished shaping of a noble statue, but I'm not going to take it home and build a life around it and live happily ever after. One, museum security would frown upon that and two, well, you just don't do that, out of respect for the art and for personal sanity.

He's my friend, officially his job title is executive protection officer, and he is here to protect me, he's not coming for my heart. Be cool.

"If I say yes, how soon can everything be legal?" I ask.

"If we run down to city hall and get the license today, we can get married tomorrow. You don't need to change your name and we'll end it whenever you want."

The mention of my name reminds me of what comes with me, what's attached to me.

"If I say yes, you have to know there are huge implications to doing this without a prenup. I don't mean that I don't trust you," I quickly add when he frowns. "But I'm putting a lot on the line and trusting you implicitly to not claim anything in the divorce."

"I won't claim anything. As long as you don't claim spousal support."

Everett's mouth quirks up in the corner and I respond with a shy laugh. I know if it was anyone else, yes wouldn't even be an option. I need someone in my corner on this thing Dad has given me to do and it's way too much to hide from him.

"And we keep it a secret?"

"Yes," he says, and he squeezes my hand. My frazzled, weary heart skips a beat.

With a nod, I exhale. "Yes."

His shoulders drop away from his ears in relief but he keeps my hand in his. In all the times he's been up in my personal space in large crowds or in mobs of photographers, I've never been able to savor his touch the way I do now. I can feel every curve and callous of his palm and fingers. His hand is just large enough to make mine feel small and protected. My heart races and I try to give it a stern talking to, telling it to calm down.

"We should go to the clerk's office now," Everett says, all business. "There may be a bit of a line."

I pull myself together and remember the reality of my publicly recognizable face.

"Just meet me back here in five," I say, "I need some sunglasses, maybe a hat."

I go in my room and shut the door behind me, sagging

back against it as I try to hold on to the feeling of Everett's hand around mine and the way he said my name in that low, rough voice.

Everett loudly clears his throat as he heads down the hall and it snaps my heart back into place. He is protecting me. There are no feelings here. I would hate to embarrass myself by letting feelings get away from me. He is doing his job. This is a job. It's all just work.

I duck into my closet and root through it to find the most inconspicuous downtown outfit I can. Jeans, a plain t-shirt, and a black baseball cap should work. Black Chelsea boots and a military green parka will complete the look. I dress quickly and check my reflection in my full-length mirror, flipping on a pair of aviators and pulling the hat down low.

"Keep yourself safe by keeping this secret," Dad said. Well, I'm about to fail, but it's a necessary fail. I need help keeping myself safe and I need to marry to do that. Deep breath. Get to the door, open the door.

Everett's already standing there waiting and I have to laugh at what he's changed into: dark jeans, an olive parka, and a black ball cap. In our quest for discreetness, we're basically matching. What is happening?

He doesn't say anything, just looks me over head to toe, smiles, then turns and walks ahead of me down the hall. Our usual routine, like nothing's changed. My gaze drifts down his arm and I catch how his fingers tap against his thumb, from pointer to pinky, counting up and down—one, two, three, four, four, three, two, one. His tell-tale sign of high anxiety. He looks down at me, a question in his eyes, and I nod to him. We're doing the right thing. He stands straighter, squares his shoulders, and opens the back door.

CHAPTER 6

THERE ARE a few couples ahead of us at the clerk's office. I pray, hope, and wish for an invisibility cloak. All we need is a tabloid writer to spot us or the wrong person to post to social media and it's game over. I don't even know how I'm supposed to look anyone in the face, carrying around everything that's supposed to be kept a secret.

"We need to get the license now and then we'll do the marriage tomorrow," Everett explains.

"Got it," I say, keeping my head down. Deep breath. "Thank you, for organizing this."

He nods to me.

Our number is called for the license and we get it no problem. I learn that Everett's never been married before, his formal state of residency is Maryland, and his middle name is Jae-won.

"Are you full Korean?" I ask. He nods without offering any further explanation. His family is...his parents are...shockingly I'm drawing a blank. Have we never talked about his family?

On the drive home, the marriage license sits on the console between us and the silence is thundering. What am I supposed to say? I can't think of anything that would be appropriate. And my empty stomach isn't making it any easier to focus.

"I'll make us food when we get home," says Everett. The way he just knows makes me want to hug him, but instead I turn my head to look out the window and shove my cheek against my fist, willing myself to keep it together. I can do this. This isn't going to be a marriage, it's simply an alliance.

As soon as we get home, fading adrenaline and rising jet lag crash over me like a tidal wave. Exhaustion has me sleep-walking down the hall with Everett's hand gently pushing against my shoulders, propelling me towards my room.

"Go, fall into bed."

I'm not going to start the steps of Dad's mission until I have Everett legally in my corner, so I can't do anything until tomorrow anyways. Bed sounds good.

"I'll bring you food when you wake up. I'll be here."

I sleep-walk into my room, toe my shoes off, and climb under the covers. Something about being home in my own bed, so fluffy, so cocooning, with my bodyguard-fiancé outside to protect me is cozy and comforting. No one is expecting me to be home yet, so no one is expecting me to work. Is this the sense of relief I was supposed to have my entire time away?

I drop off to sleep in no time.

THE NEXT MORNING is charged with frenetic energy. We're seated outside the clerks office, about to be called in for our ceremony, and as much as I'm telling myself it's just business, we're anything but business-like. Everett's fingers are tapping against each other a mile a minute and I can't stop popping the clasp on my watch. We're wearing our more typical attire, Everett in a dark suit and black overcoat, me in dark wide-leg pants, a winter white turtleneck sweater, and coordinating coat. I've popped the collar and worn my hair down in long, loose curls, a small effort at concealment.

Everett reaches over and puts his hand on my knee, shooting me a reassuring glance. The gesture is a combination of comforting and alerting. I'm hyper aware of how soft his touch is and how warm his hand is, a complete contradiction to my goosebumps and the chill in my bones from late winter in New York. I smile at him and try something new. I give him a wink of reassurance.

He grins, his whole face beaming and blushing. I would pay any amount of money for an artist who could capture that look forever.

"Next!"

We scramble to our feet and make our way to a side room with industrial carpet and fluorescent lighting. A short, round man waits for us behind a small podium.

"Do you have your license?" he asks. Everett pulls the marriage license out of his suit pocket and we both hand him our IDs.

"Alright, and do you wish to exchange rings?"

I'm about to say no when Everett pulls two rings out of his magical suit jacket pocket and hands them to the officiant. I don't even have a second to protest before the officiant launches into the ceremony.

"Then we're ready to begin. Would you two please face each other?"

I turn towards Everett, rubbing my cold hands on my coat. When I meet his eyes, I have chills, completely unrelated to the weather.

A lock of his hair is falling out of place, dipping down across his forehead, making him unbelievably more handsome and dashing. My eyes close as I take in the moment. I'm marrying him, right now, it's in progress. My dad is alive. I'm marrying Everett in secret. My dad is out there somewhere. I'm here. I'm getting married.

"Alright, repeat after me. I, Everett Park..."

I wait for Everett to say the words, but they don't come.

I look up to find he's staring down at me, speechless. Does he regret this? Is this a horrible idea after all? Maybe he's light-headed and dizzy the same way I am. I don't know how to read his expression. It's like he's never seen me before, like he woke up from a dream and found himself in this moment. I take his hands in mine and squeeze, a quiet reminder that it's just me, just Laina.

"I, Everett Park," the officiant prompts him.

Alert, on-guard Everett snaps back into place. He clears his throat and stands up straight, shoulders back, his hands tightening around mine.

"I, Everett Park," he says to a spot on the wall behind my head. "Take you, Laina Milenna, to be my lawfully wedded wife. To have and to hold, from this day forward, for better, for worse, for richer, for poorer, in sickness and in health, until death do us part."

The officiant holds out the ring and instructs Everett to put it on my left hand. As he slides it on, I don't know what I expect, but it's certainly not a stunning wide platinum band with pavé-set diamonds around the whole ring. I gasp.

"Wait," I whisper before finding my voice and saying it louder, "Wait."

Both men look at me.

"Ev, what is this?" I ask, breathless, holding up left hand. "What is this?"

He shrugs. "You needed a ring."

"I didn't think...this isn't...you don't—" I try to finish my phrase, but I'm speechless and in grave danger of bursting into tears. Why would he do something so real for such a fake wedding?

But the officiant needs to think this is a true love situation. Heaven forbid someone did leak this to the press, true love with my bodyguard would be a better spin than fake-but-legal marriage. I look down at my ring again and back up to Everett. He shrugs and gives me a small smile.

"Doesn't matter. You're Laina Milenna. You deserve beautiful things, the best things."

He nods to the officiant to continue.

"Laina, repeat after me. I, Laina Milenna, take you, Everett Park, to be my lawfully wedded husband."

I'm shaking, but I manage to repeat after him all the way through. The officiant hands me a ring and I slide the simple but masculine silver band onto Everett's hand. He flexes his fingers, makes a fist, and the ring catches the light. It's fitting for him. He looks even more attractive as a married man.

In the saddest part of my lovesick heart, I acknowledge that one day, Everett will get married for real and it won't be to me. I hope his future wife will be very happy with him. She should be ecstatic to be marrying him. He is the best man I know and deserves the very best love has to offer.

"By the power vested in me by the laws of the state of New

York, I now pronounce you husband and wife. You may kiss the bride."

I forgot about a kiss. My heart pounds as my stomach fills with butterflies. I watch Everett, trying to anticipate his next move. I don't know what's worse, leaning in for a kiss and being denied or staying still as a statue.

Everett decides for me. He takes my left hand, raises it to his lips and presses a kiss to the back of my hand, never breaking eye contact with me. His brown eyes darken and my breath catches in my chest. His soft mouth lingers for a moment and the kiss is sure and firm. There's a force behind it, an intensity and intentionality that makes my lips part in a gasp. He just kissed me. Everett kissed me.

My cheeks must be flushed neon pink and my knees are weak. This kiss to my hand has only made me desperate to know what it would be like for my lips to meet his. For a brief moment, Everett's eyes go to my mouth, then just as quickly look away.

"Congratulations," says the officiant. "Please make room for the next couple."

Right. The door of reality slams in my face. This isn't marriage, it's legal protection. My mission for Dad can start now. But how am I supposed to concentrate on anything other than Everett's lips after that kiss?

WHEN WE GET BACK to the house, all my nerves are jittery as Everett takes my coat and hangs it up. We can talk now, I can tell him everything. But first, I want to discuss the matter of the rings.

As he loosens his tie and takes off his jacket, I open my mouth to address it. Right as he starts rolling up his shirt sleeves. His wedding ring adds a mesmerizing flash of silver with each movement. Has he always done that, the whole shirt rolling thing? No, I know he hasn't. This is new and...sexy. I can't stop staring at his flexing forearms.

"Ev," I say, sharper than I intended. His head snaps up and whirls around, immediately looking for danger.

"What?"

I hold up my left hand.

"I can't go around wearing this. It's too noticeable."

His lips form a little grin that's alluring and infuriating. He's grinning like he's proud of himself.

"You can do whatever you want with it," he says.

"Everett, this must have cost a small fortune."

"Does it matter?" he asks, casually making his way down the hall. I follow him, my heels not making a satisfying click on the floor until we reach the tile of the all-white, modern kitchen. I make sure to stand on the opposite side of the island from him.

"You don't mind if I put it on my dresser and never wear it again?" I ask.

"Nope. But that's the one thing I want back in the divorce."

He grabs a glass bottle of water out of the fridge and takes a long, slow drink. I try to look away, to not take in the way his throat moves as he swallows, but it's futile. He's a magnet for my eyes.

"You can't wear yours either," I say, flustered.

"I won't let anyone see it," he says with a shrug.

I narrow my eyes at him. "Why are you being like this?"

"Like what?"

"Like nothing about this bothers you."

"Because it doesn't."

"Ev! Come on! You—" I'm about to say "kissed me" but Everett cuts me off.

"There are more important things to worry about than our wedding rings."

Our. Wedding. Rings. Nope, professionalism demands I not go anywhere near that delightful phrase.

"Right. Let's talk about what's really going on," I say.

CHAPTER 7

I LEAD us into the living room, one of my favorite rooms in the house, besides my own. The walls are a cozy deep green with one whole side of the room being built-in bookshelves, the couches are worn caramel-colored leather, and an intricately-woven red rug covers most of the original hardwood floors. I sink into a corner of the couch, folding my legs under me while Everett settles down on the opposite side, three whole cushions away from me.

Distance should mean business. Distance should mean no fluttering hearts or racing pulses. Distance should mean I don't think about how I wish things between us could have a different future.

He puts his left elbow up on the arm of the couch and leans on his fist. There's that flash of silver again. I press one hand over my heart, trying to calm it down.

My husband.

The words fill me with longing for a home of my own, a family of my own, a person to call me *"wife."* Why am I imagining a white house with green shutters and a wide porch? I'm a city girl, I don't want rural, pastoral scenes of domesticity. And yet, the longing remains.

I glance over at Everett who seems entirely unperturbed, completely unaffected. In fact, he's stifling a yawn. "Sorry. Okay, let's talk about what's going on."

Time to switch gears, no more thinking about unattainable marital bliss.

"So I'll start with what I know," he says. "A few months back, the cyber guys at Black Swan noticed that people were looking into your parents' deaths through back channels. Just asking around, probing, lots of internet searches for their death certificates. We started to connect the dots that it was all leading back to associates of the Vidovic Group. Remember the day you left for your trip, that guy in the crowd that you were worried about? He was a guy that had come up in our profiles, so your instinct was right."

"Wait, I was right? There genuinely are people who are after me?" All the blood drains from my face.

"It's okay, it's good I know what to keep an eye out for. Don't get too worried yet."

I nod, tight-lipped and terrified. "So, what's the latest?"

"The firm recently told me there's a theory going around that your dad is still alive. I got bent out of shape about it because I didn't want anyone dredging that up and I especially didn't want you to get upset if you heard about it. So I started researching on my own and found some stuff that seemed off. Then I got the case file to research The Vidovic Group and found out some more."

Could he know already? "How much more, exactly?"

Everett shrugs. "You're definitely being watched. As soon as you cut your trip short, I was suspicious that it had something to do with all that. But when I saw you step off that plane, I knew, I just knew that you had seen something. I knew you would need to say something, to vent to someone, and I thought it might as well be me. Because if you're about to say what I think you are, this is going to get ugly fast and I want to stay in front of it, to keep you safe."

The air in the room is heavy and my heart is beating a mile a minute. I shiver, partly from cold, partly from sheer fear.

"That's my end of it. Is there anything you want to tell me?" Everett asks.

"Yes," I say. My throat is dry and if I held out my hands, they'd be shaking like paper in the wind. I hope I'm doing the right thing. "It's safe to talk, right?"

"Definitely. The car is harder to secure than the house, oddly enough."

"And you swear yourself to secrecy?"

He puts his right hand over his heart. "I pledge my fealty, body and soul, to you and you only, Wife."

He says it with a shy grin, a joke to lighten the mood, but it only makes me want him more.

Everett Park, my bodyguard, all striking and handsome with his crisp white Oxford shirt, his gelled hair that he keeps running his hands through and messing up, and his earnest eyes, just called me "Wife." I've peaked when it comes to romantic scenarios and it's not even real.

But now comes the difficult task of reliving what happened in the Maldives. I swallow hard and take a shaking breath before launching right in.

"Okay, so, about four days into my trip, I went for a walk on the beach and a guy in a hotel uniform approached me. He had this huge burn on his face and I didn't recognize him until he said my name. But it was my dad."

Everett's eyes go wide with a mixture of interest and disbelief and he leans forward, nodding for me to continue.

"Dad has evidence against the Vidovic Group that was compiled by Adam Lourden, Vidovic's money launderer. There's a dossier and I'm the one who needs to get it and hand it over to one of my dad's underground associates."

I flick my fingers across my cheeks, surprised to find there are tears there. Everett's studying the fireplace opposite us, but he has the armrest of the couch in a white-knuckle death grip.

"There's a series of steps I have to go through," I continue. "But it starts with me accessing something in the family safe and then we go from there."

Tears still come, but I talk through them. "I think I'm just now realizing how traumatic that was. It's a very strange thing, to see my dad alive and know that my mom is still gone. I don't know, it's just...it's just a lot, Ev."

My heart breaks each time I relive the way Dad talked to me. One of the two people in the world I would ever look to for comfort and he didn't even talk to me like I was his daughter. It was all so confusing. I drop my face into my hands.

Everett shuffles over, the couch cushions sinking under him, tipping me towards him. He puts his arm around me and curls me into his shoulder. His other hand rests on my knee and gently squeezes, his warm gesture giving me silent permission to go ahead and let myself weep.

I cry hard, turning into a chest-wracking sobbing mess at the lostness of it all. I'm adrift in the wake of sadness and anger that's been roiled up by seeing Dad.

I push into Everett as I let the pain out and he remains steadfast, never shying away from me.

"I'm so sorry, Laina," he whispers.

It'll be okay. Dad will come back and he'll be different. Once this task is out of the way, the stress of his quest for justice will be gone and he'll be his usual self again. It'll be okay. That was a necessary, good, ugly cry, now I need to pull myself together.

Everett passes me a tissue and I take it with what I'm sure is the puffiest-eyed smile. "What are you thinking?" I ask as I mop my face.

Everett starts to say something, but shakes his head, unable to get the words out. Seconds pass by and he's speechless.

"What is it?" I ask, laying a hand on his shoulder.

He lets go of me and stands, pressing a hand to his chest and shaking his head, like he still can't believe what I've just told him.

"Do you know about my family?" he asks facing me, his expression vulnerable, his eyes sad.

A pang of guilt hits me as I rack my brain and come up with nothing. "I...I don't think so."

"Did you know I was adopted?"

"No, I didn't."

"You swear?" he asks, his eyebrows pinching together.

"I swear," I reply. "How old were you when you were adopted?"

"I was a baby when the Lourdens adopted me."

"The Lourdens," I piece it together and gasp. Everett is studying his shoes. "Your parents were—" another thought hits me, totally out of place, "You're the heir to the Lourden fortune and you're a bodyguard? You must be rich, you—"

Everett cuts into my thoughts with a piercing look. "I didn't have a good relationship with my parents, at the end. I refuse to bear their name. I haven't heard someone say it directly to me in over a year. It's not the happiest moment for me."

I bite my cheek as shame makes me flush hot.

"I'm so sorry, Everett. I had no idea."

"It's okay, it's not your fault."

He exhales heavily, and in a few strides he crosses the living room, heading for the hallway. "You want me to cook you something?" he asks, hooking one hand behind his neck, lingering in the doorway. One look at his pleading expression tells me it's not about me at all.

"Sure, whatever you want."

He tilts his head towards the kitchen and I accept his silent invitation to come with him. It's an honor to be asked to witness Everett in the kitchen. He's a wonder with food, but after close observation over the years, I've learned he works his thoughts out through cooking. This is about him processing, not about culinary delight.

I sit on the barstool at the island as Everett moves around gathering dishes, utensils, ingredients, and spices. I wait until he's cracking eggs to ask the question that's worrying me.

"Did you know? About what he did for the Vidovic Group?" I say quietly. "I wasn't the first one to tell you that, right?"

"No, no, I knew." he replies, reassuring me. "I found out he was laundering money when I was in high school. It's what led to me leaving home for good as soon as I graduated. Never spoke to them again."

My shoulders sag with relief, but also more shared sadness. "How did you find out?"

He huffs with disgust, shaking his head. "A few of Vanya's mercenaries broke in one night and kept us at gunpoint for hours while they beat up my dad." Everett whips the eggs with excessive force, pausing only to add a splash of milk. "I'll never forget hearing my mom cry that way. We were incredibly vulnerable and I hated it. And then to learn it was all because of my dad's greed."

More pieces of Everett fall into place. It makes sense how he could go from a traumatic event like that to wanting to be a bodyguard. To wanting to know how to protect himself and others. He reaches for salt, smoked paprika, and pepper.

"I'm so sorry, Ev," I say.

He braces himself against the counter and sighs, then looks up at me with a hint of tears catching the light.

A wave of tenderness crashes over my soul. I want to hug him so tight, to heal him where he's hurting. I wish it was my role to console him, to embrace him, to be there for him. I may be his "wife," but I still don't have license to act like it.

Everett pushes away from the counter and moves to the stove, talking to me over his shoulder. "Things were strained in our family from a young age. Dad had a golden path for me, to be ready to take over as CEO once I had my MBA. There was a timeline and everything down to the month."

"You were meant to be CEO of Lourden Luxuries?" Although it sounds strange at first, I could see it. Everett has such a commanding presence, yet he's likable and easy to talk to. He'd probably be amazing at running a company like Lourden.

Everett shakes his head, raising his voice over the hiss of

butter hitting the skillet. "I never wanted it, it was just my dad's dream. Once I pieced together what he was doing, I decided to cut myself off from my parents, especially from him and his money and his plans for me."

"But..." I start, not knowing where I want to go with my sentence. Everett pours the egg mixture into the pan with another wide hiss and uses a flat whisk to stir it.

I should just stop talking at this point, let him be. He folds the whisk through the eggs until they cook into a fluffy pile of creamy goodness. Everett puts some sourdough in the toaster, chops chives to sprinkle on top of the eggs, and brings two plates of eggs and toast over, setting one down in front of me with a fork.

I take a bite, closing my eyes and savoring the flavors of a dish as simple as scrambled eggs, but prepared to perfection.

"Good?" he asks.

"The best," I murmur in response. I've died and gone to culinary heaven, but I feel that way every time Everett makes me food.

We don't say a word until we finish every speck of food on our plates. I wash the dishes and let the soapy, hot water soothe my senses, leaving Everett to his own thoughts.

Without my asking, he comes over and takes a dish towel from the front of the stove and starts plucking items out of the drying rack, wiping them down, and putting them away. He moves next to me, silent and sure, just far away enough that we don't even brush up against each other.

The way we've just shared secrets, the way we're going through sadness and loss and pain together is special, and I'm overwhelmed by how right it feels. But the secrets also hurt, like pushing on a deep bruise. At least we have each other right now, we're not alone. For how much longer though? My chest goes tight as I fight to keep my emotions at bay.

When the last dish is dried and put away, Everett leans back against the counter alongside me, crossing his arms over his chest.

"I did not know my dad was a mole. Everything I thought I knew...it throws it on its head. I wish I could talk to him, get some closure, but..." he trails off as emotion takes over his voice.

"Ev," I say, taking a few small steps closer to his side. I have to hug him. I have to. He's my friend and I love him and he's hurting and there's no one left to hug him but me. As a friend.

I hesitantly ease my arm around his waist, watching to make sure he doesn't flinch, that a side hug is the right thing right now. He puts his arms around my shoulders, leans his head to rest on top of mine. His body relaxes until we're both holding each other.

We've never stood like this before, but we fit perfectly. The heat running down the side of me that's pressed to him makes my body hum with awareness. I can hear his heartbeat and I hope he can't tell how my own heart is trying to run away. It's just a hug from a friend.

Who happens to be my husband.

"Let's go see what we find in the safe," he says.

CHAPTER 8

THE HIGH-TECH FAMILY safe used to be in my parents' closet. My small selection of jewelry sat alongside Mom's diverse array of bracelets, necklaces, and earrings, all encrusted with rubies, emeralds, pearls, and sapphires. Dad's diamond cufflink collection took up a whole shelf in the steel box.

But after they died, I didn't want to have to walk through their room just to access it. Their room is frozen in time. Their clothes hang in the closet, their perfume and cologne sit on the dresser, the book Mom was reading is on her nightstand with a bookmark near the halfway point. I don't like to go in there anymore.

I swing open the double doors to my own closet and stare at the wall opposite me, where the family safe is now mounted. I've added my own expensive watches to it, but otherwise everything is the same. It's coded to biometrics for my dad, my mom, and me.

Everett and I stand in front of the safe, arms crossed, looking at the metal box a little bigger than a microwave.

Everett studies it with an experienced eye. "I was here when you moved this. There wasn't anything suspicious."

What if Dad was wrong? What if he's delusional?

"Do you have a scanner with x-ray vision that you can wave over it to find a heat pattern or something?" I ask.

Everett chuckles at my suggestion. "I'm no Ethan Hunt."

"Who?"

"Ethan Hunt? *Mission Impossible*?"

"Is that a movie?"

Everett's jaw drops.

"Laina Katarina Maria Genovia America Milenna, you've never heard of *Mission Impossible*? How?"

I shake my head, grinning at how personally offended Everett is. About two years ago, he found out I had two middle names (Annalisa Freya) and thought it was absurdly comical. So when he's making a point, he strings together as many words ending in "A" as he can.

"Okay, well, now you have to watch it, because that's basically what we're doing right now. A quest with a MacGuffin."

"A McMuffin?"

"A MacGuffin, an arbitrary thing that we're after, the thing that will complete the mission. Like in *The Pelican Brief*."

"The Pelican—"

A scathing look from Everett cuts me off. I don't dare admit I've never seen that either. Who knows how many more names he can come up with.

"I'll just open the safe," I mutter.

Family safe, social security number, false bottom, wait for instructions. I'm anxious for this to be over, to get Dad back, for all this tension and danger to dissolve.

I step forward, rub my palm on my pants, and hold it out. Right as I'm about to press down on the screen, Everett grabs my hand, his thumb brushing across my knuckles. He opens his mouth and pauses, like he wants to say something, but can't find the words.

"You okay?" I ask.

He bites the bottom corner of his lip and exhales a shaky breath while staring down at me. I meet his questioning look with one of my own. I'm not that much shorter than him, but I always seem very small compared to his imposing, powerful stature. He lets go of my hand and I straighten my shoulders not backing down from his stare.

Then he has the nerve to run his thumb over his bottom lip and I'm mesmerized. All reasonable thoughts are gone as I watch him trace his lip.

"This is not going to go the way you think it's going to go. If the dossier is in there, that means all your dad said is true and that means there will definitely be complications somewhere along the way."

I don't hear a word he says. All I can think about is how those lips felt pressed against my skin.

"Hey," he says, getting my attention. I instantly blush. "What are you thinking about right now?"

"What are *you* thinking about?" I retort like a six-year-old.

He quirks an eyebrow at me, then shakes his head.

"I'm wondering if I can talk you out of this."

"No, this is important and necessary. I do this, I get my dad back. And that's the purely selfish reason."

"What are your other reasons?"

"Because my dad asked me to. It's important to him. And it was important to your dad too. And it's important to all the victims of the Vidovic Group. Ev, there are so many suffering people out there who need our help. I mean, ultimately, it's important to the whole world."

"Laina, is it more important than you dying?"

I wave off his concern. "My dad said there's no imminent threat to me. He made it sound like I'd be flying under the radar."

Everett reels back. "What?" he practically yells. "He said you'd be flying under the radar?"

Am I remembering Dad's words correctly? He made it seem like it was a little dangerous, sure, but not deathly dangerous. Yeah, flying-under-the-radar dangerous is about right. But Everett takes my hesitation as a bluff and he scoffs, crossing his arms over his chest, all his muscles flexing. Uh-oh, this is his pissed-off look. His eyes flash with anger and he leans forward, enunciating every word.

"Laina, he straight up lied to you."

"Excuse me!" I say, recoiling. "My dad doesn't just go around lying to people."

"He would to get what he wants. Which in this case, seems to be blind vengeance."

"Everett! That is a horrible snap judgement!"

"If he cared about anything else, he would have come straight back here, back to you, the minute he walked out of that plane crash."

"He—"

My retort catches in my throat. What? No. Dad has a perfectly good reason for what he's doing. It's stopping a criminal warlord. It's righting wrongs. It's a well-thought-out plan, not blind vengeance.

"Laina," Everett says firmly. "I understand. It's your dad. You worship your dad—"

Enough with this casting-doubt shtick. "Hold up, did you marry me in order to help me or not? Why do that and then try to talk me out of this?"

"I had no idea about this secret mission thing," Everett holds his hand up in the air in innocence. "I thought maybe you would have some new information about the Vidovic Group and I wanted to be aware of any threats that might have been made against you. I did not know that you were determined to put yourself in harm's way."

"Isn't that why you're here?"

"No, Laina Amelia Caledonia Beretta Milenna, it's my job to make sure you stay out of harm's way."

I don't so much as bat an eyelash at his attempt to lighten the mood. Everett takes a breath, then switches to a pleading tone. "I have to keep you safe, away from danger."

The back and forth, the emotions of the day that have been swirling around me rear up. I shake my head to clear my thoughts, but Everett takes it as me saying no.

"People died!" he says, raising his voice just enough to make his point. "My mom, my dad, your mom, they died for this. And when someone comes after us for this dossier, it's going to be you or me. And I'm not going to let it be you."

The fight is knocked out of me at the implication of what Everett, my bodyguard, is saying.

"That's ridiculous," I whisper, then clear my throat. "You don't have to die to protect me."

"But I would. Every single day, I would take a bullet for you, I would do whatever it takes to keep you safe."

"No job, no career, no salary is worth that," I reply.

Something snaps in Everett. His self-control runs out. He lunges forward and swoops his hands to either side of my neck.

"You are, Laina," Everett says, his face close to mine, full of conviction and unfeigned emotion. "You are worth that."

There's a flash of honesty that passes between us, a lightning crack, a new awakening. It illuminates something that I've never seen before, something I've been blind to up until this point. Could it be?

"No," I whisper in surprise, delight racing through my veins as my heart pounds. Could he—?

Everett drops his hands from my blushing cheeks and turns away before I can get another look at his expression. But I could swear what I saw was real.

I'm not the only one holding back *feelings*.

As much as I want to dive into that fact and relish it and respond to it, if that's the case, I understand how carrying out this mission where I'm potentially in danger would be asking a difficult thing of him.

There's a lot going on between my dad and the news about his dad and this dossier. Allowing feelings to come towards the surface would only complicate things further.

I come around Everett to face him. "I promise to be as safe as I possibly can," I say solemnly. "I promise not to put myself at unnecessary risk. I promise to listen to and do everything you tell me to do."

He arches an eyebrow at me. "Everything I tell you to do?"

My face flushes. "You know what I mean. But yes, please, help me do this."

Everett studies my face as I give him my most entreating look. Finally, he nods.

I go straight to the safe and press my right hand to the scanner, then punch in my social security number. The safe pops open with a new chime, a sequence of beeps I haven't heard before. Everett helps me move all the contents to the bench in the middle of the closet, our fingers occasionally reaching for the same item, our shoulders skimming past each other.

"Okay," I say, stepping up to the empty safe and running my hands over every surface. "How do we find the false bottom?"

"You look for the Brazilian butt lift," says Everett.

I glare at him in disapproval. "Horrible, horrible joke."

Everett grins. "I have a magnet handle in my cache. We should be able to lift it off."

He jogs out and as soon as I know he's down the hall, I shake my hands in an attempt to tame my nerves. This is insane. I can't deny what I saw in his eyes as he tried to talk me out of this. I can't let go of the subtext of his words. He would take a bullet for me, he thinks I'm worth that. I press my hands to my cheeks in an effort to cool my blush.

Everett comes back with a circular magnet the size of a saucer with a handle on the back. When his eyes meet mine, there's about a million things I want to do with him and none of them involve taking apart a safe. But he's in a completely different mode of thought, focusing on the task at hand.

"Give this a go," he says, handing the magnet to me. "Set it on the floor of the safe, then press that power button to activate it."

It snaps onto the bottom of the safe and I press the button, then give it a wiggle.

"Woah, that's never coming off."

I pull and nothing happens. I brace my legs wide and flex my nonexistent core muscles to help. I pull again, my neck bulging as I hold my breath.

Nothing.

One more time.

I reposition my grip and give it my all.

"Five, four, three," Everett is barely whispering.

My hands fly off the magnet and I jump back with a yelp. "Why are you doing a countdown? Is there a bomb?"

"No, no, sorry! No, nothing's wrong, go ahead."

I glare at him and try to pull the magnet one last time. Not a thing happens. I swear not even an atom shifts.

"What the heck?" I say, letting go. "Why would—I mean... it's just—ugh," I finally snort-growl in frustration.

"There it is," says Everett. "I was doing the countdown to your cute little snarl."

"My snarl?" I ask, panting and bracing my hands on my hips. "I don't snarl." But I take the "cute" as a compliment and tuck it away.

"Only when you're incredibly frustrated," Everett replies. "It's rare and adorable. You kind of did it after the meeting with Noa Ice."

I scowl at him, then point to the magnet. "You try."

Everett steps up and grips the handle of the magnet, his forearms flexing. His biceps engage, then his shoulders strain at the seams of his dress shirt. It's clear that he's putting all his effort into this. I hold my breath, hoping he's strong enough.

"I have faith in you," I say quickly.

Veins in his neck are straining and his face is turning reddish purple when an awful screech blasts through the closet. Nails on a chalkboard is too nice of an analogy, this sounds like a fork on a dinner plate but ten times worse.

"Yeah!" I cheer as Everett pulls the metal plate all the way out of the safe and lowers it to the floor.

"Oh my gosh, why is that so difficult?" he says, panting. "You could have never done that yourself. Now I'm sweating." He swipes his sleeve across his forehead in a move that's unfairly attractive.

I've followed the steps and this is it, the moment of truth. I look inside, anxious to see the famous dossier.

"There's nothing in there," I exclaim in disbelief.

"What?" Everett comes up behind me to look. He's so close and his citrusy cologne smells like it's mixed with sheer masculinity, but it's probably just Everett's sweat. Unfairly delicious.

"There's nothing," I repeat.

I back away from Everett as he fishes out his phone and taps around. The open safe looks like it's yawning, empty and taunting me.

"What's going on?" I ask. "There's supposed to be something there. Why isn't there something there?"

"If I knew, I would tell you," Everett says under his breath. He's paying close attention to his phone and the closet is growing smaller and more suffocating the longer he stares at his screen.

"Why is this going wrong from the get-go?" Fear of failure is wrapping around my heart in a tight spiral. "What if Dad was delusional? What if he never comes back?"

"Easy, Laina, it's okay."

"No, it's not. This isn't okay. I'm failing already."

"Listen to me, Laina," Everett looks up from his phone, straight into my eyes. "You followed instructions perfectly. You are not failing. Trust me, you're okay."

He waits for me to nod and exhale before he looks back to his phone.

"Can we go out and get coffee or go for a run or something?" I ask. "I need some fresh air."

"We can't really afford to go traipsing around the city right now," Everett says.

"What if we're disguised?"

"You can't be that disguised with what we have on hand."

"You don't have like a magical costume-mask-creator thing or something?" I ask.

He narrows his eyes at me. "Are you sure you've never seen *Mission Impossible*?"

"Positive."

"Okay, I've got something," he says, looking back at his phone. "I think removing the false bottom wasn't to get something, it was to activate something. Lifting the bottom turned on a beacon."

"A beacon? What for?"

"I'm assuming that's how someone's going to get in touch with you. I asked Black Swan for cyber support and they just let me know there's a signal coming from the house."

"Oh. The next step is wait for instructions," I admit. "I just thought there would be something there."

Everett shakes his head and slides his phone in the pocket of his slacks.

"I don't think the beacon is secure, unfortunately. Anyone can see it. You're right, this closet is getting stuffy," he says, and I can pick up a hint of stress in his voice.

I lead the way to exit the closet, only to hear Everett's low voice by my ear.

"I'm going to sleep with you tonight."

CHAPTER 9

I wheel around and firmly brace myself inside the doorframe, blocking Everett's path.

"No."

"Yes," he retorts, like there shouldn't be any argument.

"Everett Park, just because you are my husband does not mean you get conjugal rights." On this point, I'm emphatic, pressing my finger into his firm chest. I draw the line at consummating a fake marriage.

He goes wide-eyed. "That's not what I meant. I just need to be closer to you."

I raise my eyebrows.

"Not like that! I meant on the floor or like on that weird couch thing," he says, pointing to the cushioned window seat. He does his best to sound annoyed, but there's a telling redness sweeping up his neck. "I would rather be here than down the hall and around the corner if someone breaks in and tries to hurt you."

"Oh." I lower my arms from the doorway. Everett brushes past me and as I study his overly-attractive back, before I can slam my hand over my mouth or tell myself to stop talking, I impulsively, stupidly ask, "Out of curiosity, just reflecting over the last few years now that you're leaving, have you ever wanted to sleep with me?"

Everett halts, then slowly turns towards me, a smoldering grin catching me off guard. My face flushes red.

"Is that the kind of conversation you want to have?" he asks. His eyes are dark and looking down at me from under arched eyebrows.

"Wait, no, I didn't mean—"

He takes a step closer, closer, until we're chest to chest and I have to tilt my head all the way back to hold my ground and stare back at him. My legs are wobbly and my lips part as I suck in a breath, waiting for what he's going to do or say next.

"I can answer that question, if you want."

His body is heated against mine and my blood is on fire. Any last shred of professionalism or friendship would be incinerated if he said yes. And I'd be devastated if he said no.

"Don't answer," I say.

"Are you sure?"

"Positive," I whisper, weak and wavering.

He leans down, so close that I can feel each word he says as breaths against my mouth. "Then don't ask questions you don't want to know the answer to, Laina."

He has the audacity to give me a rakish grin that makes me desperate to kiss him as he slowly backs away from me.

We need to calm down, take a step back, do something to distract ourselves. Something without beds and sleeping. I can't even admit to myself how much I want to know the answer, but once I do, either way there will be a ripple effect and so much to unpack. I won't forget the moment that passed between us earlier, but now is not the time. Tomorrow, I'll revisit this tomorrow. Right now, we need to lay low, stay firmly in the friend zone.

"You know how you're leaving soon," I say. It's hard to admit, but it's true and I need to face the truth.

"Yeah?" Everett says, his expression clouding over.

"I was just thinking, we've never done anything fun together. We've never like gone to an arcade or seen a Broadway show or watched a baseball game."

"Laina," Everett laughs and shakes his head. "I'm not the person you have fun with."

"Who else do I have fun with? It's not like I have a deep bench of friends."

Everett's look is tinged with pity, but I push past it.

"Can we watch a movie together? *Mission Impossible*? We already have to wait for further instructions, so might as well have some fun."

"You want to have a movie night?" asks Everett.

"Mmhmm, a comfy movie date, I mean night. Comfy movie night," I say, biting my bottom lip with anticipation and silently pleading for Everett to go with it. I see the moment his gaze drops to my mouth. I fold my hands under my chin and add, "Please, Everett, I haven't watched a movie in forever. It'll be the perfect distraction."

He looks at me, tilting his head to one side, like he's trying to judge why exactly I'm adamant about this. Or maybe he just thinks I've lost my mind.

"Fine, but I'm going to go change," he announces. "I'll meet you in the den in a few minutes. You said the attire is comfy movie night?"

"You have clothes other than white Oxford shirts and dark suits, right?" I tease.

"You'll see," he winks at me. I don't know what that means, but I hope it means he does in fact have other clothes. I'd hate to have things get weirder by Everett waltzing into the den half-naked. I would *hate* for that to happen.

I CHANGE my pants for leggings, but keep my turtleneck sweater on. I grab more water from the kitchen before making my way down the hall to the little navy-blue den with the oversized leather sectional and big screen TV. Dad always worried about the design aesthetic not being quite right to match the rest of the house's old money, mid-century modern decor, but Mom said her love language was large, overstuffed leather couches and recliners to curl up in with a good book, so of course Dad acquiesced.

The remote is right where it should be on the TV stand, and I'm surprised the batteries still work. I haven't had time to sit down and watch a movie in forever. Everett's heavy footsteps come down the hall towards the den and I'm equal parts curious and nervous. What am I about to lay eyes on?

Everett enters wearing dark gray joggers and a short-sleeved black t-shirt, barefoot with a gun in his hand, screwing on a silencer. My jaw drops. He sets the gun down and reaches to scratch his left shoulder, pushing his sleeve up, showing me a stalking, snarling tiger tattooed in bold blacks and grays covering his entire left bicep and shoulder.

I didn't know I had a type, but this is now officially my type. Tall, handsome, fills out a t-shirt way too well, knows how to handle himself in dangerous situations, and a striking tattoo I didn't know he had under all those suits and ties. No, forget that, it's not a type, it's just Everett. This guy, this is the one who has my heart.

"Laina," says Everett. I finally meet his eyes to find him grinning at me with a raised eyebrow.

"What?" I try, but I can't look away from his biceps.

"Are you drooling over me?"

"Ev! Stop making it weird," I say, trying to navigate the smart TV to search for the movie before I combust.

"I'll stop when you stop looking at my arms like you want to lick them."

"I am not," I protest, still sneaking glances at his sexy body.

"You know what, I'll save you the effort of fighting off your temptation and grab a sweatshirt. It's cold in here."

Well, there goes the greatest view in the history of my life.

Everett comes back pulling a tan hoodie over his head and now his hair is thoroughly messed up. As he sits down next to me, I can't help smiling and boldly reaching over to run my fingers through his hair, trailing my nails against his scalp. He hums in approval.

"Your perfect hair is no longer perfect," I tease. His hair is like thick threads of black silk slightly matted together with gel or pomade. I've always wanted to see him like this, lounging in casual clothes with unruly hair, and I love it more than I care to admit. It's a version of Everett only I get to witness.

"You should probably stop doing that," he says in a low, deep voice as my fingers stay in his hair.

"Why?"

His eyes flutter closed and he smiles, whispering to me. "You're driving me crazy, Laina."

I short-circuit. My breath hitches in my throat and my hand freezes in place.

Everett grabs my wrist, lowering my hand back to my side. "And I can't afford to lose concentration any more than I already have." He opens his eyes, his dark and heavy gaze meeting mine, then looking to my mouth. "I can't mess this up," he says, articulating each word with conviction.

I don't know if he means his assignment as my bodyguard or something about *us*. The way his eyes are fixated on my lips makes my head swirl with anticipation, but his body is tense. Are we ready for the guardrails to come off? Now that he won't be my bodyguard, does this mean we should risk it all? But the timing feels way off and it won't be right until the waiting and this task is all over. We have time.

"I don't want to mess this up either," I say quietly. "What we have, our friendship, is so special to me."

Everett looks away, his face clouding over, and runs his hand through his hair. Shoot, I should not have said 'friendship'. Why did I do that?

As his hand drops back to his side, I notice he's not wearing his ring. Of course. He said he wouldn't. It's best to keep things professional for the time being. Casual, but professional. I quickly move away, mentally and physically.

"Let's watch a movie," I say, clearing my throat and trying for a more normal tone. "Let's watch a movie, eat some food, wait for further instructions like the super-secret spies we are."

I press play and the mood settles back towards our normal levels of friendship. The movie is a classic '90s action movie, but at one point Tom Cruise delivers a very emphatic line about everyone being dead and it's so overdone, I can't help but giggle.

"Laina Cordelia Diana Lasagna Grenada," Everett murmurs, playfully shoving my shoulder. "You did not just laugh at that."

"I did and there's nothing you can do about it," I say, pushing back on him with full confidence.

Everett suddenly wraps his arms around my torso and squeezes. It's like being tangled up with two giant boa constrictors, and I realize that he might be thinking about trying to tickle me. I grab his hands and try to fight him off, but he's so strong, he holds on to me with an ease that is almost primally attractive.

Are we like teenagers, using a fight as an excuse to touch? Absolutely.

The front doorbell rings and I freeze.

Everett instinctively jumps up, grabs his gun, clicks a bullet into the chamber and motions that he's going to check it out and for me to stay in place. He goes into full action mode, holding his gun with both hands, sweeping the hall before silently moving towards the front door.

I would get up and follow him, but fear has paralyzed me in place. I can't move, even if I wanted to. I shut my eyes and press my hands over them. The silence is so loud. My pulse is pounding in my ears and all of my body feels numb.

Then Everett shouts back to me. "Laina, it's okay. It's just Ainsley." Ainsley? There's the click of the gun decocking followed by rasp of the front door unlocking.

"Hello, Evvy," Ainsley's voice rings out loud and clear down the hall.

My adrenaline makes me feel like I'm bleeding on the

inside of my skin and even though I know the suspense has passed, I don't trust myself to get off the couch. There are footsteps down the hall towards me, then Ainsley comes into the den, brandishing a neoprene laptop case. Everett is glowering behind her, all trace of laughter gone.

"What's up?" I say, my voice cracking.

"You are supposed to still be on vacation," says Ainsley, handing me the laptop in its case.

This is it? It's such a slim, skinny thing. I was expecting a steel briefcase or a fireproof safe or something. And I can barely wrap my mind around the fact that Ainsley, my personal assistant and secretary of three years, has been holding on to this in secret.

"Just wanted to make sure you had everything you need over the weekend," she adds.

I look over at Everett and he seems equally shocked. He's running his thumb over his mouth again, his other arm folded across his chest. We're both trying to piece this together.

"Is this everything?" I ask.

"Yup, should all be there," says Ainsley.

"All this time—"

Ainsley cuts me off, waving her hands across her throat.

"I don't know what that is and I don't need to. But I'm here for you if you need anything," she adds. "Oh, and Everett, Boss finally did the paperwork and that contract is in your inbox."

Everett clenches his jaw and opens his mouth, probably about to say something scathing to Ainsley, but with a quick squeeze to his tiger tattoo, she waltzes down the hall and out the front door. Everett follows and locks up after her.

"What was that?" I shriek when he comes back.

Everett shrugs. "I think she's a co-agent of mine."

"She's like a sleeper cell bodyguard?"

His furrowed forehead and flashing eyes tell me he's clearly unamused about being kept in the dark. "I didn't know. That one totally surprised me. I'm going to have to talk to my boss about it."

The way Ainsley talked to him as she left, the one word she said keeps running through my head.

"What contract?" I ask Everett.

"Hmm?"

"Ainsley said there's a contract for you."

"We can talk about it later. Let's deal with the laptop."

I want to push him to talk about it now, but my curiosity and drive to help Dad win out. I turn the laptop over in my hands and pull it out of the case. It's thin and cold, space gray, smooth as I run my hand over it.

"Wow, this is it. It's a lot lighter than I thought it would be."

I check my watch, trying to judge how much daylight we have left. Everything always feels more tense in the night, so if there's any way to get this done before the sun goes down, I'm all for it. I wonder if just opening the laptop triggers another beacon or if there's a message or if I put in a fingerprint or something.

"Is that beacon that you noticed from the closet still going?" I ask, opening the laptop.

"Yeah," he says, his fingers counting against his thumb as he watches me. "You're just going to go for it?"

"Yep, just going to go for it."

CHAPTER 10

I PUSH the power button and there's a low hum as it boots up. The screen goes black and a dialogue box appears, one of those old school black screens with a blinking green cursor. I hit enter. It types out a message, "Please enter the first three fingerprints of each hand beginning with the left thumb."

As I press my fingers on the little power button that doubles as a fingerprint scanner, creeping thoughts of dread enter my brain. *What if this is a bomb? What if this is all part of a scheme that's actually for evil, not justice?*

But I go forward with it. I'm committed now. Once it's scanned the required prints, the black dialogue box goes away and a white screen appears. Nothing else changes after that. Just a bright white screen.

"What's happening now?" I ask Everett, pivoting the laptop so he can see it too.

"My guess? Someone's been notified and is now setting up a meeting location and time."

"The right person, right?"

Everett shrugs as if it's anyone's guess and his lack of surety makes me nervous. "We might be waiting a while, but don't close it."

I scan the room for a safe place to set the laptop down and seeing the gun with the silencer on the side table reminds me we're not in normal life by a long shot. I make room on the opposite side table and angle the laptop towards the wall so the bright screen isn't blinding us, but I can see if something changes.

I'm about to start the movie when Everett puts his hand over mine. "Maybe we should talk about me leaving, about why I'm leaving."

The temperature in the room seems to dip another ten degrees as icy fear settles in my stomach. I don't want to talk about it out loud, as an actual event that will actually happen.

"How about after the movie? Or tomorrow?" I say, suddenly eager to avoid this conversation for as long as possible. Denial is my strategy and fear is fueling it.

"Laina."

"You told me at the airport," I remind him. "It's what's best for you and your career."

"And you believed that?" he asks. "Let me clarify—"

"Look, this is supposed to be our fun movie night," I emphasize. "It's already been interrupted once, let's get back to making a good memory."

I hit play and a palpable blockade goes up between us. It's cowardly, I know, but I'm afraid that one badly-worded sentence, one truth that touches a nerve, will throw our entire relationship haywire. We'll have the conversation and see what follows, but I want something happy and just for us before that happens.

We finish the movie on our own sides of the couch, the

playfulness gone. Everett wordlessly gets up and goes to the kitchen and I don't follow. After a while, he comes back with two plates full of grilled cheese.

"*The Pelican Brief*?" He asks and I put it on. We don't interact any more than that.

Tears sting my eyes when the end credits roll. It's dark outside now and there hasn't been any messages. Everett is quiet and in his own world of thought.

That was it, our one "fun" movie night, never to be repeated. Before a few days ago, I never considered the possibility of a life without Everett, and now it's haunting me with its emptiness. I should have been braver, should have been more honest with him, with myself.

I reach over to make sure he's still there and my hand settles on his, resting on a pillow between us. I lace my fingers through his and squeeze, unable to hold back a sniffle.

"I'm a little scared of the future. I'm really going to miss you. And a tiny part of me feels like you're abandoning me."

In one swift movement, Everett scoops me up onto his lap. He hugs me to him, his arms tight around my waist. I wrap my arms around his head and neck and hug him back.

"Laina," he whispers, heartbreak in his voice. "The few days you were gone, it was like half of me was missing. Leaving you is the last thing I want to do."

I take his face in my hands and press my forehead to his. Maybe I misjudged this, maybe this conversation about him leaving is exactly the one we need to have. I gather my courage.

"I don't know how to be without you," I whisper. He inhales sharply and his hands tighten at my sides.

The explosive sound of breaking glass echoes through the

house. I freeze in his arms, clinging tightly to his neck like a terrified child.

"It's okay." He gets us to our feet in a burst of strength. "Get the laptop."

I move somehow, snapping the laptop shut and holding it against my stomach. In a whisper no louder than a breath, Everett gives me instructions. "We're going to your closet, stay low and stay with me."

"Why my closet?" I whisper back.

"There are no doors on this room and I swapped your closet doors for bulletproof ones years ago." I noticed they were heavier after my parents' funeral and I always chalked it up to grief making everything stand out in starker contrast.

Nope, just bulletproof doors.

Everett pushes me behind him. He clicks a bullet into the chamber, holding his gun at the ready.

Adrenaline courses through me and my fight-or-flight reflex is on high alert. I put my hand on Everett's back and even through his sweatshirt I can tell every muscle in his body is taut, tense.

We creep down the hall, half-hunched. We pause in the hallway, to the left of my bedroom door. So far nothing seems out of place. When we swing around the doorframe and charge into my room, Everett keeps me pressed up against his back, using his body to shield me. I poke my head out to the side just enough to see the scene. There's cold air hitting my face. Something's not right.

We came in too fast.

There's an intruder in all black with a ski mask on, crouching on the windowsill next to the closet, a puddle of broken glass on the carpet below. Everett startles, caught off-guard. I would scream, but like a horrifying nightmare, my mouth opens and no sound comes out.

The intruder pulls something from a holster and hurls it at Everett. In a glint of moonlight, I see a thin throwing knife, sailing in a clean line towards Everett. I don't have a chance to react before it sinks straight into Everett's left shoulder. He shouts, swearing loudly, and drops the gun as he uses his right hand to cradle his left arm.

I crouch down and do my best to frisbee the laptop across the floor, praying it slips right under the bed, out of sight. It slides under the dust ruffle and now I have two hands free.

And then I glance to the side and see the intruder lining me up in their sights, another knife in their hand.

I crouch behind Everett as he slumps forward, grab his gun from where it landed the floor, aim for the intruder's knee, squint my eyes, and pull the trigger. I can barely hear over the sharp crack of gunfire, but judging by the bellow of agony that follows, I hit my target.

The intruder starts to fall backwards out of the window, then they tap something on their chest and they're yanked up and out of sight like a puppet on a string.

Everett is breathing hard and I'm in disbelief that what just happened actually happened. I run to the window and try to look out and up to see where the intruder's gone to. Are they on the roof? Were they dangling from a silent helicopter?

A strong arm wraps around my waist and tugs me backwards out of the window, just in time, barely missing the volley of bullets that rain down.

Everett's managed to drag me out of the line of fire, one-handed. He just saved my life.

Everett and I are both panting, my heart is pounding, and

I feel warmth coming through my sweater. I look to see where it's coming from, wondering if I've been shot, if I'm going numb, not feeling it.

I run to flick on my bedside light and it's worse than I thought. Everett is leaning against the windowsill, bleeding badly from behind the knife that's buried in his shoulder. Blood has soaked through his sweatshirt and onto me.

"You okay?" he asks as I run to his side.

"Yeah, I'm good. You need to sit."

"I'm gonna pass out," he breathes, leaning hard on me. "Put pressure on it, leave the knife," he nearly throws up just saying the word. "Call 911."

"Easy," I say, wrapping my arm around his torso and bracing my legs to lower him to the floor. I lean him against the wall and run to my closet to grab the nearest piece of fabric. So what if it's a limited-edition Hermes scarf? I remember enough from high school anatomy and physiology to know this wound needs to stop bleeding or he's going to lose too much blood.

"Laina," Everett whispers. He's so pale in the moonlight. I take the scarf, wrap it around his back and under his armpit and silently thank the injury gods that there's just enough room for me to cinch it tight between his heart and the knife.

I don't hold back as I tighten the makeshift tourniquet with all my might and Everett roars out a swear word.

"Just pass out, you'll feel better," I say through gritted teeth. "I'm getting your phone."

I reach in the pocket of his joggers and find his phone. I don't think, I just call. I don't care how many paparazzi get wind of this, how many gossip papers run this as a front-page story, how many people see or hear us, all I care about is taking care of Everett. He needs immediate medical help.

I leave the phone on speaker as the dispatcher walks me through the timeline. Everett is still conscious, but he's shaking and I know that's not a good sign.

"The knife, it had to be a knife," he says through gritted teeth.

"Pretend it's a dolphin or a seagull or something," I whisper to him as I try to follow the instructions for putting more pressure on the wound.

"What?"

"Pretend a seagull was looking for a fish and they thought your body was an ocean and they took a nosedive into your shoulder."

"I can't. I can't." He's getting more worked up and I am desperate for the ambulance to get here. I don't know how much blood he's lost and I don't know if the knife hit a major artery or vein inside his body and all I can think is that I cannot watch him bleed out. I cannot watch him die.

"Everett, my guy," I grab his face with my bloody hands and kiss his forehead. "It's okay, I'm here."

"I failed you," he whispers, his breath washing across my lips. "I'm failing you."

"You did not fail. I'm safe, I'm okay. You protected me."

He tries to swallow, but he's fading faster and faster. I know that he'll probably be fine, he's going to get light-headed and that's okay, but a cold web of fear is spinning tighter and tighter around my heart. He'll probably be fine, but he could also very well not be fine. He might not make it.

"Everett Park, you cannot leave me a widow," I say, grasping for the darkest humor, tears falling down my face as ambulance sirens draw closer. He finally gives in and passes out and I stay with him, pressing both my hands to his chest to try to slow the bleeding until I hear the paramedics pounding on the front door. I rush to open it and hurry back to show them where Everett is, slumped over and lifeless.

They take over and I stand back alone, shaking, watching them make quick work of getting Everett on a gurney and out the door. I follow close behind and they load him in an ambulance that's already flashing its lights. As they're about to close the door, I step onto the bumper, determined not to leave Everett.

"Family only," says the paramedic.

Relief washes over me. "I'm his wife." The guy hesitates. "Would you like to go down to city hall and check the records?" I snap. He nods me in and I take a seat.

The moment I sit down, everything blurs. My senses dull as someone asks me a question.

"What?"

"How did this happen?" asks the other paramedic, a female who's checking out the handle of the knife.

"Home invasion," I say.

The male paramedic has just said Everett's going to need a blood transfusion.

"Do you know your husband's blood type?"

I shake my head, feeling ashamed, while everything is replaying in my mind like a movie.

Everett saved my life when my stupid self decided to look up and out the window to see where the intruder came from. He pulled me back, despite his pain, and I narrowly missed being shot in the head. He did his job to the utmost and I have to believe he's going to be okay.

The trip to the hospital is quick but harrowing. The way the paramedics communicate never shows any kind of hope or despair, it's all neutral medical talk.

"We're going to take him in to surgery when we get to the hospital. Does your husband have any personal belongings on him?"

I'm going numb now as I watch them cut off Everett's sweatshirt and then his t-shirt, leaving his pale, muscular chest exposed. And right in the middle of his sternum rests his wedding ring on a silver chain.

If I thought I couldn't live without Everett before, it was merely a reliance based on function. But as I bury my face in my hands and sob, I know that I need him because he is everything to me.

CHAPTER 11

THE DAY I met Everett was so odd. The first half and the second half were from two different worlds. In the morning, I went to a conference as a sort of ambassador for The Milenna Company, but mostly I wanted to start making my own connections in preparation for my personal business plans.

I tried to dress the part of a smart CEO, and I remember feeling so badass in my navy cape and tall black boots paired with an office-appropriate sheath dress. My sleek ponytail was swishing as I walked and I thought, "This is what it's like to be a chic, uptown businesswoman with the world on a string."

I headed home on a high, wanting to recap the event with my mom, but remembering that she and Dad were on their annual anniversary getaway to Paris. I had a whole empty afternoon in front of me and I thought I might read a book or even watch a movie.

I stepped inside the comforting entryway of home and shut the door, the carpet runner muffling my heels as I headed to my room.

But Mr. Delancey stepped out into the hall, giving me a

heart attack of surprise and stopping me in my tracks. He didn't say anything, just waved me over, his face undecipherable.

I followed him into the living room to find an army of Milenna PR, legal, and media associates congregating on our leather sofa and green velvet armchairs, hovering over the marble coffee table. They were all on edge. I scanned the faces of people I vaguely recognized. They seemed scared, worried. No one was looking at me.

There was a tall, Korean guy in a dark, fitted suit standing near the bookshelves. He met my gaze and held it. His eye contact wasn't full of sparks or sending off warning bells in my head. Instead, it was comforting. I appreciated someone acknowledging my presence in the room.

"What's going on?" I asked.

"Laina," said Mr. Delancey, without looking at me. "Your parents—"

I immediately felt an absence in my chest, like someone had pulled my heart out, a cavernous ache hollowing out behind my ribs.

Mr. Delancey came closer, taking my hand in his for a moment before I snatched it back.

"Tell me."

He tried to clear his throat. My patience was running out when he finally spoke. "Your parents were in Paris, but they... they died in a plane crash over the Alps. We just got word. There was a fire. No survivors."

People around me were breaking out in sobbing and weeping and I knew in my heart what was happening, but my body and my brain were accepting it in slow motion. I scanned the room again. No one said anything to me.

I looked at the guy in the corner and he straightened up and came over to where Mr. Delancey and I were standing. Even in my heeled boots, he was taller than me by a few inches and he blocked my view of the rest of the living room like a wall.

"I'm so sorry," he said in a low, smooth voice. His eyes told me his sympathy was genuine.

"Thank you," I managed to exhale.

"This is Everett Park," explained Mr. Delancey. "He'll be your executive security from now on."

"My what?"

"I'm your bodyguard," said Everett. And that was about the last thing I heard.

I remember going straight to my room, calling my parents, and listening to their voicemail greetings over and over and over. I fell asleep at some point and woke up to an empty house, the sun sinking, making the shadows long and the hallway dark. I walked down the long hallway to the kitchen and traced my fingers over the multitude of family pictures that lined the walls.

When I made it to the kitchen, I turned on the light and jumped. Everett was leaning against the counter, without his suit jacket, tie flipped over his shoulder, eating cereal. He stood up straight and set the bowl down on the counter, wiping his mouth.

"I'm sorry," he said, "I was really hungry. I don't know what the etiquette is."

He was basically standing at attention and I realized I was his boss now.

"It's okay," I answered. "I'm glad you helped yourself."

I got a glass bottle of water out of the fridge and let the water soothe my dry, parched throat.

"If you're okay with it, I'd like to do something for you," Everett said. I leaned back against the counter, hugging my arms across my chest. I had taken off my boots at some point, but I was still in my dress. I didn't know when I would change, didn't know if I wanted to.

"Like what?"

"Can I make you dinner? I'm decent at a few things."

"I don't know if I can eat anything."

He nodded. "The day I found out my parents died, I forgot to eat all day and then I woke up in the dead of night super hungry and it was the most depressing thing I've ever experienced."

My eyes welled with tears for him. He knew, he understood, but I wished he didn't. I wished no one did.

"I'm sorry," I whispered.

"We're orphans," he said with a shrug.

It struck me as morbidly funny and I smiled. "When someone says orphans, I picture little Victorian children at a train station with a brown tag pinned to their jacket."

"It is kind of a dramatic word," he said, giving me a sad smile back.

I nodded, sniffling.

"I'll bring dinner to your room, if you want," he offered.

"That's really kind of you."

I turned, water bottle in hand, ready to head back to my room, when something occurred to me.

"Why do I need a bodyguard? Do you live here now?"

Everett was already opening drawers and cabinets, rooting

around the pantry, and checking ingredients in the fridge as he talked.

"Mr. Delancey hired me. You're going to be CEO of The Milenna Company. A lot of attention will be on you for a while. I don't have to stay here, unless you want me to. It must be hard to suddenly be alone in a big house like this. I noticed there's a guest suite near the back of the house, that could work for a bit."

I couldn't speak. I couldn't hear. I couldn't feel my limbs.

"Wh-what?" I stammered. "I'm CEO?"

Everett stilled. He turned to face me.

"You didn't hear it from me," he said, a guilty expression on his face.

"Stay," I whispered as a final request.

I turned and somehow made it back to my room, falling on my bed to stare up at the ceiling. The mantle of leadership was going to be laid on my shoulders and my parents wouldn't be there to help me, support me, comfort me. I was alone.

At some point, Everett knocked on the door and I said he could come in. He set a bowl of spaghetti on my desk and said something about being in the guest suite. Everything had changed before I was ready. I was terrified.

CHAPTER 12

I DON'T KNOW how much time passes, but I exist in a terrified daze in the emergency waiting room. Someone draped a warm blanket over me. A nurse brought me some tea. Everett's phone is in my pocket, his blood crusting on my white sweater. His silver chain and ring are around my neck. I'm so grateful I never thought to take my ring off.

But someone to the left of me is holding their phone at a weird angle and I realize they're either videoing me or taking a picture. I'm going to attract attention here.

I pick up Everett's phone and guess the password based on what I remember seeing him type in. The phone unlocks as another person to my right raises their camera, this time more obviously. I find the number I'm looking for and dial.

"Ainsley, I need your help."

I tell her where to find me and why and she comes blazing in less than fifteen minutes later. She goes wide-eyed when she sees me.

"Oh, Laina. Okay, let's get you to the car," she says, ready to escort me out.

I shake my head and stay put. "Everett's in surgery. I'm staying here."

She nods. "Let's go somewhere more private."

I slowly stand up and follow her, my body aching from the absence of adrenaline. The room she finds for me has a small cot and a chair and I lay down on the cot, prop my hands behind my head, determined not to fall asleep. Ainsley takes the chair and attends to something on her phone.

"How are you?" she asks softly.

"Worried," I reply.

"He's a tough cookie. He'll pull through for you," she says. "Where's the laptop?"

"Under my bed." I turn my head to look at her. "How much do you know?"

"Enough to know we need to secure it."

"How are you part of this?" I think to ask. "Is Mr. Delancey in on this too?"

"No, Everett and I work for the same parent organization, Black Swan Protection Agency. Our boss saw that Everett wasn't following normal protocol with you—"

"How so?" I cut in.

"He never took time off, he refused to show up for annual training in person, he insisted on being the only one assigned to your detail."

"I guess I just thought that was all normal bodyguard stuff. That he was just doing his job really, really well."

Ainsley laughs and shakes her head. "And you thought it was normal to be waited on hand and foot? That he would have your favorite coffee for you at 2 p.m. every afternoon? That he would ask me to put fake meetings in your calendar that were always canceled so you could have some downtime?

That he would always hold your coat for you, carry your stacks of files, get every door and elevator for you? You think that's what bodyguards do for their bosses these days?" She's not irate, she's genuinely curious if this is how I think. "Laina, he worships the ground you walk on."

"Don't say that," I whisper. I don't want to hear this from Ainsley. I want any conversation about this to be between me and Everett, alone. We deserve that.

Ainsley must not have heard me, because she presses on. "Anyways, once Everett was too deep in his feelings to be your security, he was essentially compromised. So when your executive assistant position opened up, my boss put my name forward as a candidate and we just hoped and prayed you'd pick me."

"And Everett never knew?"

"Nope. I played up my crush on him to throw him off guard, because I do have a crush on him. He's the most gorgeous man I've ever seen in my life, and I lived in Seoul near the Blue House. Have you seen the presidential bodyguards there? They're hot, but Everett's hotter."

I give Ainsley a look of sheer incredulity. She's talking about *my husband* and how attractive he is while he's in surgery for a life-threatening injury. She catches my look and hunches her shoulders in apology.

"Sorry," she says sheepishly, "Got carried away there."

"How did you get the laptop in the first place?"

"Your dad was old friends with my boss. I think my boss was your dad's security detail at one point in his life."

Of course. My dad and his old friends.

"My boss gave the laptop to me when I came to New York and said that I was to keep it safe and hand it off if I ever got a text about it. I didn't know what was on it until after I brought it to your house, then I got the whole spiel from Boss. Big stuff."

"So what happens now?" I ask.

Ainsley eyes me in my bloody, frazzled state. "How much do you want to finish this? Because there's always the option to not go any further."

I shake my head. "It's not an option."

"I assume you know there are huge risks involved with trying to end a criminal group," Ainsley says.

I knew, but there was no way to truly know. If I could have foreseen this, would I have made a different choice?

Guilt presses on my chest for what it's cost Everett. Even with the blood transfusion, even if he's stabilized, is his shoulder going to be okay? Is he going to have full mobility? Or will nerves and muscles and ligaments be severed beyond repair?

"Okay, well, I'll go back to the house, deal with the clean-up, and get the laptop." She stands and I nod my approval of her plan.

I close my eyes, but all I can see is Everett's pale face, his eyes rolling back in his head. I shiver, haunted.

Ainsley reaches for my hand and gives it a warm squeeze, then leaves.

Silence descends and now I notice my ears are ringing. Probably from shooting a gun without hearing protection. I check my watch. What time did we get here? How long have I been awake? It doesn't matter, I refuse to rest until I know Everett's okay.

A NURSE SHAKES ME AWAKE.

"Mrs. Park?" she asks. I look up at her in confusion. Oh, yes, I'm Mrs. Park. I sit up fast, seeing stars for a moment.

"Is he okay?" I ask, my voice hoarse from lack of proper sleep and an excess of crying.

"Yes, come with me."

I'm hugging myself, cold and worried, as I follow her down the halls. As we pass a window, I can see the sky getting lighter. We've been here all night.

The nurse has to use her key card a few times to open up different automatic doors and it gives me reassurance that we'll be safe here. No one can get to us without hacking a few systems, which should be some deterrence.

Finally, we stop in front of a light oak-colored door. She gently knocks and eases the door open. All I can see is the foot of the hospital bed, the rest is behind a green patterned curtain.

"Go on in," she whispers. "He's probably resting. He came out of anesthesia perfectly, but he'll be tired for a bit. Call me if you need anything."

The door closes behind me as I tiptoe towards the bed. I brace myself for what I expect to see: gore and pale skin and bloody bandages. But there's none of that.

Everett is upright in the hospital bed, his head turned to one side, sleeping peacefully. There's a white sterile bandage wrapped around his shoulder and chest, a sling securing his arm against his torso. He's shirtless, but his skin is clean, looking healthy and faintly tan again. The tiger's paws are barely visible under the edge of the bandage.

The relief I feel is so complete, it's almost tiring. He's made it. He's okay.

There's a large chair next to the bed and I slip into it. I hug my knees to my chest and study him for the longest time, taking in the sight of his rising and falling chest, his smooth skin, his steady heartbeat on the monitor.

Who would I be without Everett and how can I ensure I never have to find out?

He stirs, his eyebrows pinching together in pain, and I move to sit near the foot of the bed on his right side, suddenly shy. His eyes flutter open and he looks around, confused. Until he sees me.

"My girl," he whispers with a smile, his expression relaxing. "You okay? That's just my blood on you, right?"

I smile and nod, wiping my teary cheeks. He looks so gentle and soft, so different from how I last saw him.

"You doing okay?" I ask.

"The pain meds are working."

He holds out his good hand and I lean closer to take it in both of mine. I relish the warmth of his skin and the surety of his grip. The chain around my neck slides forward and his ring hangs between us.

"Oh good," he says with relief. "I was wondering where that went."

He traces the chain to the back of my neck. "I want it back now, please."

I set his phone down on the bedside table for him and grin as I slip the ring and chain over my head. I stand and lean over him to put it around his head.

"Obsessed much?" I joke as I sniffle. He smells like antiseptic and sterile cotton. I want his old smell back.

"Mmhmm, very," he says. "The nurse said my wife stayed here the whole time I was in surgery. Obsessed much?"

"Definitely," I whisper as I kiss his broad forehead, pushing his hair back the way he likes it.

His heart monitor beeps a little faster, a tell-tale sign that I'm not the only one feeling something, something like love, care, and affection.

His eyes flutter closed.

"I'm pretty weak," he admits. "But I want to help you finish the job."

I shake my head. "Don't think about that right now. I'm just glad you're okay."

He sighs and I can tell he wants to counter and say something, but he's not strong enough yet.

"I'm going to sleep with you now," I say. That gets a faint smile from him before his heart rate drops back down and he's asleep again.

True to my word, I push the chair right up against the hospital bed, recline it as far as it goes, and fall asleep watching Everett's heart monitor unfurl in steady lines.

CHAPTER 13

Hours later it's officially morning and the first person to come barreling into Everett's room is the last person I expect. Mr. Delancey.

He wakes me up with a too loud, "Good morning."

I peek out from under a thin blanket with a groan and see Everett sitting up in the hospital bed, setting his phone down, looking like he's been awake for awhile. Everything about him seems healthy and whole, such a contrast from last night. The human body and its ability to recover is remarkable.

Everett sees me stirring and winks at me. I wink back, sliding the blanket down so he can see my grin. My entire body fills with butterflies.

There's a conversation waiting to happen. All the subtleties need to go, I want to talk about what we've been holding back. Watching him bleed out reminded me that time is fragile and short, and I need every second I have remaining with him to be filled with honesty.

He glances up at Mr. Delancey, who we've both completely ignored since he entered the room.

"How are you doing, Everett Park?" asks Mr. Delancey. He sounds concerned, but there's some passive aggression in the way he just used Everett's name.

"Fine, sir," says Everett. "The surgeon said my shoulder should heal completely, no permanent damage."

"Good, good, that's good news," says Mr. Delancey, pacing at the foot of the bed. He pauses and his eyes flick back and forth between Everett and me, narrowing in suspicion.

"Have you seen the news?" he asks me. I shake my head as Everett nods.

"What news?" I stand and stretch, looking between the two of them.

"We'll get to that," says Mr. Delancey. "Look, I have to ask, are you two married?"

"Yes," we answer in unison.

"Bloody hell," he murmurs under his breath, rubbing his hands over his eyes. "Why on earth would you do that?" He's almost pleading in his tone. "I'm sorry, I know that Everett is hurt and I'm so glad you're going to recover and thank you so much for protecting Laina. I'm so glad you're both safe. But why did you two go and get married? Especially without telling me?"

His "not angry, just disappointed" tone is my kryptonite and it's eating me up that I can't tell him the truth.

I can't tell him the real reason, that I needed a legal ally, that now Everett can't testify in court that my dad is actually still alive. I also can't tell him that I'm trying to hand over evidence to take down a criminal group and I needed my bodyguard to be on my side. I can't say that I needed a confidant, a teammate, a friend. And I certainly can't say that Everett is turning into something more than all those things.

I'm hesitating to answer Mr. Delancey and I know it looks bad.

"Are you pregnant?" he asks, gently.

"No!" Everett and I say at the same time, a blush taking over my face and neck. Everett chimes in, "Getting married was a decision we made together." Good answer, Ev.

"Okay, but why?" Mr. Delancey asks again.

Everett and I have a silent conversation with our eyes, one where I freak out a bit and he gives me reassurance that the truth stays between us and he's in my corner. The outcome is me saying, "This is a completely personal and private matter."

Mr Delancey scoffs. "Geez, do I have to get you guys in front of a lawyer to pry this out of you?"

Well, jokes on him, because not even that would work.

"What did you see on the news?" I ask Everett, shifting focus.

"All the paparazzi stuff from last night," he holds out his phone towards me, but as I reach to take it, he pulls it back. "Just so you know, it's not great."

I keep my hand outstretched and he hands the phone over. I google my name and scroll through the headlines.

Not great is an understatement. There's speculation about everything from Everett heroically rescuing me during a home invasion to rumors of domestic violence perpetrated by me, a stone cold—wow.

"As you can see, this is fairly awful for you and the company," adds Mr. Delancey.

"So?" I say with a defensive shrug, casually handing the phone back to Everett while shaking on the inside. It's bad, one of my fears come to life. The vitriol, the shaming, the names are terrifying. And Dad's going to come back to this.

"So? *So*?" Mr. Delancey says, a hint of drama rising in his voice. "The board is wondering if you're fit to lead the company. They've been chomping at the bit to boot you out and put in one of the old guard ogres. Influencers are starting to cancel you over the domestic violence speculation, not to mention the memes and deepfakes and AI-generated B.S. that's going to come of these photos of you covered in blood."

Everett quietly swears next to me. I'm attempting a shrug when Mr. Delancey straightens up and says, "This could be the end of your term as CEO, Laina."

"It's not like I wanted this to happen," I press back with a loud voice. I look at Everett, gesturing to his bandage. "I didn't purposefully ask Everett to get a knife shoved in his shoulder."

"That's not the issue. It's one thing to have your bodyguard go to the hospital, it's another to say you're his wife. That's the part that is making the most waves. You made a decision in secret that has far more implications than you're realizing."

"Like what?" I say, jutting my chin out, shoving my hands under my armpits to hide the shaking. I'm doubling down in all the wrong ways, but I can't stop. I want to defend Everett and I want to defend our decision, but now it's looking like Dad is going to be helping clean up my mess, something that only happens in my nightmares.

"Did you sign a prenup?" asks Mr. Delancey.

"No. I trust Everett."

Mr. Delancey sighs. "Yeah, we're going to need some lawyers involved. Everett has claim to half of your net worth now, he could wipe out the company if he wanted to." He looks to Everett. "I'm not saying you're going to do that, I trust you too. But the board and the company have a right to be worried."

"How can we reassure them?" I ask, going into business mode. There's got to be a solution. There's a fix, we just need to name it and implement it.

"Laina, you have enemies in the business world. I've shielded you from a lot, but you should know that making a singular rash choice to marry in secret without any legal protection means you are now vulnerable to all kinds of attacks on your character and your ability to lead a global conglomerate. You are the CEO, you do not get to make choices in the heat of the moment, especially involving yourself with Everett. But since that ship has sailed, you are going to have to deal with the consequences."

I look over at Everett and he won't meet my gaze. Instead, he's counting his fingers against his thumb, his forehead furrowed with worry.

"Is this because he's my bodyguard?" I ask. "Would it have been different if he was another CEO or, I don't know, a prince of a small European nation? Is this because he works for me? Is it a power dynamics thing?"

"It is so much more than that," Mr. Delancey counters. He raises a pointed finger at me and inhales like he's gearing up for a dressing down.

"Hey, easy on her," Everett cuts in.

Mr. Delancey shoots him a glance, then deflates. "You know what, Laina, this is a highly emotional time and I'm sure you're tired. We'll continue this conversation later today."

My anger goes through the roof and just as I'm about to tell him off and possibly fire him, a nurse walks in the room and we pause the conversation. The tension in the room hangs heavy as the nurse pokes around Everett's bandage and checks his temperature and blood pressure.

"You seem to be doing well," she says in a sweet bedside manner. "And there's no sign of fever, so I'd say you'll probably be able to go home soon."

It's good news, but I don't even care, I'm so pissed off. I face towards the door and try to scrub the heat off my cheeks. I'm embarrassed and ashamed.

I pick up Everett's phone again, scrolling through the headlines. The judgement towards Everett and me is starting to sting now. He doesn't deserve it. I'm just trying to do the right thing. But there's no way to correct anyone's perception of it. For now, perception is reality.

The nurse wraps up and leaves and I'm not sure what to say or where to begin.

"Turn your phone on," Mr. Delancey says. "I'm going to do some ground work and make a few calls, then I'll be in touch for your statement. Be prepared." He leaves, closing the door gently behind him.

Rage and indignation stick in my throat and those are just the surface emotions. Deep down, I'm petrified of losing the influence I have at The Milenna Company. Things could go from bad to worse in hours. Dad could come back to a company that's tanking, all thanks to me.

Not just that, there are loads of awful things being said about Everett that make me livid.

"Laina," Everett's tone is asking me to turn around and look at him. When I do, I keep my gaze on the foot of the bed.

"I'm so sorry," I whisper.

"Laina, you need to think about what your statement is going to be."

My eyes snap to his.

"The rest of the world does not care about what you've done right or wrong. They don't care about me, they don't care about you, they want to turn you into a villain and tear you apart. You need to do what's right for you."

"What are you saying?" I ask.

"I don't need protecting," Everett says. "I am still leaving. I got the email from my boss that my contract is finalized and signed. So, do what you have to do, say whatever you need to say about me to protect your position."

"I am not going to throw you under the bus, Everett. Absolutely not," I say.

Everett's eyes go soft and tender, but he shakes his head. "You have given everything to being CEO, you live and breathe Milenna, you cannot throw that away. You have to keep your influence as a leader."

He's breaking my heart. He sees me and may be the only person who does. And he's decided to leave. I bite the inside of my cheek, refusing to cry anymore today.

"I haven't even asked, do you know where you're going next?" I ask in a stupid, fake-perky voice.

He sighs and the look of pity mixed with regret is awful. "I'm going to Poland."

"Poland!" I shout. "What?"

"I'm sorry," he says in a whisper and now he's getting choked up.

"Why are you doing this?" I ask, coming closer, ready to sneak up under his good arm and hold on to him forever.

Everett sighs. "Come here."

He waves me over and makes room for me next to him on the bed. I come around and sit down on his right side. We're shoulder to shoulder, hip to hip, so close I can listen to his breath. Everett takes my left hand, gives it a reassuring squeeze, and after a moment, he gently twirls my ring around my finger. It's familiar, intimate.

"Look, this isn't about me right now," he says. "We'll talk about me once things are more sorted with you. I just want it to be clear that you don't have to protect me. I knew what I was getting myself into when I asked you to marry me, how I could get hurt, how painful it could be, how it could go wrong. But I underestimated the way it would play out for you professionally if people found out. That's on me. So, spin this however you need to."

"Don't fall on your sword," I say. "Don't sacrifice your dignity for me."

Everett clears his throat and presses on. "I'll cooperate gladly with whatever story you go with, no matter how it paints me. I never wanted to jeopardize your position."

Part of me melts at how considerate he is and part of me is angry at how the fight's gone out of him.

"Mr. Delancey will probably want us to get a divorce," I throw out, hating myself for testing the waters. Everett doesn't deserve underhand tactics. But I want to know, I need to know if he's going to just let me go.

"We both knew from the beginning this wasn't supposed to be forever," he says in a grave voice. He sounds dead serious, but something about his words flies in the face of everything that's transpired.

I want to protest, but I'm cut off by a knock at the door and Ainsley waltzing in with the laptop in her arms. I jump up and stand a foot away from the bed.

"Good news, I found your laptop!" says Ainsley, faltering

a bit when she sees Everett. He's leaned back, running his hands through his hair, closing his eyes. He looks like he needs a nap. "Wow, look at you, Evvy. Your sex appeal is going to go through the roof with a hot scar on your shoulder."

I pointedly clear my throat. She's not wrong, somehow he looks even more handsome all haggard and bandaged than he does in his suit and tie, I just don't like hearing another woman say it. All rights reserved, by me.

She tosses him a black zip-up hoodie she must have picked up at the house. He grabs it before it hits him in the face, giving her an exasperated look.

"Well, aren't you happy I'm here?" She asks.

Everett nods reluctantly. "You're on the detail now?"

I pick up the hoodie and drape it over Everett's broad shoulders as he leans forward, then eases his good arm through one sleeve. He murmurs a quick thanks. It's such a little thing, but it's something that makes me feel wifely.

"Yeah, until Garth gets here. You're lucky it's him and not one of the hot ones like Erik or Lucas or Jack. Less competition for you."

"Garth?!" I exclaim. When Everett said someone would replace him, I just assumed someone in the same vein of life. A late twenties, early thirties guy who looks nice in a suit and gels his hair. Garth sounds like—

"He's so nice," murmurs Ainsley in reassurance. "He's this big ol' Montana cowboy. He's got the cutest grandkids."

Garth sounds like he might wear a blazer, jeans, and cowboy boots. Not that I'm judging. And did she say, "Grandkids?"

"Yeah, cute ones. Laina, here's some clothes for you too." Right, I'm in dire need of a shower and a change of clothes.

"Anyhow, about this," Ainsley holds up the laptop. "We need to talk next steps, because you're on the front of every tabloid and TikTok ForYouPage, which makes things a little complicated as far as where and when you're seen."

"And with who," interjects Everett.

I'm so irritated by all the hype and the mess that other people are creating around this. "Why do people do this? Why do people mass together and make these group decisions about what a person is allowed to do or not do and it's not even about people who are evil or mean or wrong? Like why is all the energy directed at me and a marriage certificate? How about we go after the gross, evil, shadowy people in the world?"

I point to the laptop. "This is what matters, so I'm just gonna open it up and restart the signal process and we'll hand it to whoever's responsible and move on. This already feels like it's dragging on."

"Wait, let's at least get back to the house," reasons Everett. "It's good we have it with us, but don't do it here."

Judging by the headache pressing into the back of my eyes, we could all use some rest, food, and water.

"Okay, let's go back to the house and go from there," I concede.

It takes a bit of time for Everett to get discharged and in the meantime, I make use of the bathroom to shower and change into the joggers and sweatshirt Ainsley brought me. Once we're cleared to leave, she sneaks us through some back hallways and an empty ambulance bay to a waiting car.

She slips into the driver seat while Everett and I sit in the back. As we pull away, I turn and see that the whole front entrance of the hospital is swarmed with independent journalists, paparazzi, and reporters. I'm thankful for being spared that right now, but I'm going to have to make a statement sooner rather than later.

I run my hand over the cover of the laptop, a touchstone of reality. This needs to end, this emotional dance with Everett, this threat to all of us, this weird liminal space. The laptop is real and the evidence my dad has compiled is important. I have to remind myself that I'm doing this for all the victims, all the grieving people who have been hurt by this criminal organization. Yes, I have a selfish motivation, but I'm also doing this for justice's sake. I'm going to see this through.

CHAPTER 14

WHEN WE GET BACK to the house, the three of us make our way into my room. I brace myself to find blood stains on the walls and broken glass all over the floor, maybe a bird nesting on my bed. Instead, the cream carpet is completely spotless and the window entirely replaced. It's eerily clean.

"How did all this get fixed?" I ask Ainsley, my jaw dropping in disbelief.

"Oh, called in some favors. Boss went to college with a guy who's a cleaner on Long Island. He said this was an easy one. He dealt with law enforcement too. It's handled."

By "cleaner", I gather she doesn't mean a Molly Maid housekeeper.

Everett gingerly lowers himself to sit on my bed, his left arm now cradled against his chest in a black sling, the empty sleeve of his zip-up sweatshirt hanging limp at his side. He makes himself comfortable, leaning his back against the headboard, and I sort of love the picture it makes. Until he grabs a pillow and presses it over his face with a groan.

"You okay?" I ask.

"He's gonna need his meds soon," Ainsley says, "They should be waiting at the pharmacy, I'll grab them."

"Ains," says Everett, putting the pillow to the side. "Thank you. We'd be sunk without you."

Ainsley beams and does a little hair flip over her shoulder as she leaves.

"I'm going to restart the message screen," I say, sitting down on the edge of the bed, the laptop balanced on my lap.

Everett nods for me to go ahead and I open it up. I repeat the process of entering my prints with annoyance, ticked off at the intruder for interrupting and forcing us to start all over. It goes to the bright white screen and I set it on my desk to wait.

"I'll get you some water," I murmur, heading to the kitchen.

As I pass down the hallway, my gaze sticks on a photo of Mom and me at the first Irene Milenna Opera Foundation Gala. I must have been about fourteen and I insisted on doing my own makeup. It doesn't look great.

Mom was so encouraging that night. She never pushed me to the side, never acted like I was an inconvenience or embarrassment. She included me in every conversation, whispered behind-the-scenes anecdotes, and smiled at me all night long. I remember it as the night I became my mom's best friend.

My dad and I never really had that. I was always striving to win, like I hadn't quite achieved the same status as him. There was always a sense that there was something else I needed to do, someone else I needed to be, despite his assurances to the contrary.

Everything was supposed to be all pretty and orderly for his return to Milenna, but now this stupid media attention is messing things up. And I still don't know how things are going to end with this laptop. I keep dangling the promise of freedom to myself as a reward, but there are no assurances of that until I can talk to Dad about how things will be going forward.

When I come back to my room, Everett's holding out his phone for me. "Mr. Delancey. You forgot to turn your phone on."

I grimace as I take the phone from him, bracing myself for whatever comes next. "Yeah?"

"Laina, someone's gone down to City Hall and dug up your marriage license, so that's just fantastic. We need your statement now."

I rub my forehead and try to rack my brain.

"What line would you go for?" I ask Mr. Delancey, hoping he's feeling gracious.

"Wha-What line would I go for? Laina, you're the one who got married, you know the reason. I don't get what the big secret is. Why can't you just say the reason?" Mr. Delancey asks incredulously. Then he lowers his voice. "Did Everett coerce you into something? Do you need a lawyer? "

"No, definitely not. It's nothing coercive. I just...it's between Everett and I, and I don't owe the public any more than that."

Mr. Delancey exhales loudly through the phone. "There are basically two options for explaining a quick, private marriage. Uh, you can disavow, basically say it was a drunken mistake or something like that. Or you go full lovebirds and say you've both secretly been in love with each other for years and it was a romantic decision."

"Neither of those seem right."

"Well, pick your poison, Lainey. Get that to me in five minutes, so I can get it to Legal before we go to the press."

He hangs up abruptly and that act alone puts true fear in my stomach. Mr. Delancey is never abrupt.

"You heard that?" I ask Everett.

"Yeah. Like I said before, say what you need to."

I tap Everett's phone against my chin and keep going back to the phrase "marriage of convenience." It's not like Everett needs a visa, it's not like this is about healthcare benefits, although that's a perfectly valid reason for a lot of people. It's not like he needs to marry to inherit a kingdom.

Then it hits me. A valid reason that could not only work for me, but might help Everett as well. *Please let this work.*

"Ev, did you ever review your parent's will?"

"No," he says, rubbing his eyes. "I think the lawyer tried to call me, but I never wanted to know."

"You need to get in touch with your dad's lawyer, right now," I say, pushing the phone against his chest. He shoots me a pinched expression of annoyance.

"What?"

"If we're lucky, there's a clause in there about something that only happens once you get married."

Everett looks at me like I've well and truly lost my mind, but I press on.

"If there happens to be an article or clause or whatever that says you get money or an inheritance of some sort when you get married, it could be very convenient for us. I could spin it as mutually beneficial and show that you're not a threat to the assets of the company."

"Laina, I don't think...I would not get your hopes up. And that logic doesn't even sound right."

"Can you at least try?" I ask, urgency rising in my tone.

"We didn't have that kind of relationship," Everett says, swinging his legs over to sit on the side of the bed. He groans and grabs at his shoulder, swearing under his breath. "Once I left, I left, and I'm pretty sure they said good riddance to the back of me. No. The answer is no."

"What if you believed a lie?" I ask him. "You said yourself that you wanted to get more closure than you have. Maybe this will be it."

"And maybe it won't be."

I pace at the foot of the bed, biting my lip, trying to really think it through before I push for this even harder.

"Ev, I understand the comfort zone of feelings. But in order to move forward in any way, we're both going to need to kick our own butts out of our comfort zones."

"Who's kicking butts?" asks Ainsley, waltzing back in with a paper bag that she rattles in Everett's face.

"Laina is kicking my butt," he mutters, grabbing the bag and dumping it on the bed. He fiddles with attempting to unscrew the white lid off the plastic bottle before I gently take it from him and hand him back a responsible amount of painkillers. He shoots me a thankful glance and washes them down with some water.

"Do you need anything else?" he grumbles at Ainsley. She raises her eyebrows and slowly backs out of the room, closing the door behind her.

His phone rings and I can see Mr. Delancey's name on the caller ID. Everett immediately smashes the red button, ignoring the call. It seems like a point in my favor, but I know he'll just call again. Everett can't stop rubbing his eyes. Poor guy has been through the wringer these last couple of days.

"I'm sorry that I'm asking you to do this on my timeline, in a way that benefits me," I murmur quietly. "I'm sorry. I can understand you're very upset."

He's quiet for so long, I worry what I'm going to hear next from him. Is he done with me? Am I too much? Is this all too much? Is this the final straw that's going to send him packing without another word to me?

"Kittredge, you've never seen me very upset."

I bite back a grin of relief. It's the one line from Mission Impossible I distinctly remember and I take it as a sign that he's going to call. I go to him, stepping between his legs, to hug him tight against me. He wraps his good arm around my waist and the warmth of him is so comforting.

"I don't deserve you," I whisper to him.

"Sometimes you really don't," he whispers back with a laugh.

"Thank you, thank you, thank you," I say as I pepper his hair with kisses. "I know I'm asking something crazy and costly. So thank you."

He pats my hip and I nearly dip my head down and kiss him right there. My fingers brush across his cheek and he looks up at me with heart-melting eyes as his hand moves up to linger on my waist.

Standing here like this, looking into the best brown eyes in the world, feeling the sheer force of years of friendship compounded by desire and genuine care, wanting more than just a passing moment of passion, wanting a lifetime of it is reaffirmation.

I am so in love with Everett Park, my bodyguard.

And he's leaving me.

CHAPTER 15

I TAKE the laptop with me to the kitchen to give Everett privacy to make his call and find Ainsley rummaging through the fridge.

"You don't keep much food around do you?" she asks. I set the laptop on the counter and take a seat on a barstool.

"I mean, there's food, but Everett is the chef. He's the only one who knows how to make a meal out of this."

I pick the cuticle around my thumb while tapping my foot against the footrest. The nervous energy that's been latent is now pushing up into my chest and I desperately want to burn it off. I want to run and work through the biggest question of all—why is Everett leaving and how can I get him to stay?

"Do you think we have time to go for a run?" I ask Ainsley. She shoots me a look that tells me I'm crazy for asking. "What?"

"Laina, do you know how much press is after you right now? You want to go for a run?"

Right. Forgot about that. Time is moving in a weird way now, the tension making each minute seem hours long.

I wonder how Everett is doing. I don't want to go check on him and make him feel like I'm nagging, but I'm also wondering how many times Mr. Delancey has called him and what the repercussions are going to be.

"You got something." Ainsley announces, pointing to the screen.

My stomach drops as I read it out loud. "1700 tonight, downtown helipad 3, Laina must accompany the laptop to the drop. Pass phrase required."

Adrenaline pumps through me. I remember the code my dad told me and I mentally chant *It's snowing in the Black Hills*. This is it, where the plan takes me out into the open. This is the scary, real stuff, the stuff I've only seen in movies. I'm about to go take a laptop to a helicopter to stop a bad guy.

"We've got about an hour then," says Ainsley. "Get some food, do whatever else you need to do. I'll go with you. We'll leave Everett here, he's in no condition to handle something like this."

"What happens if this dossier ends up in the wrong hands?" I ask. "Should we do some sort of decoy or try to copy the contents of it onto a back-up?"

Ainsley makes a face. "Eh, I have a feeling it would require computer skills above my pay grade. We have a guy back at Black Swan that could do it, but we don't have enough time. A decoy computer case at least may not be a bad idea though. We'd have to work with whatever we have here."

"I might have something in my room, or we can look in my dad's office."

Ainsley nods. "It'd be good to give you something more than your fists. I'll see if Evvy has some weapons for us."

"Speak of the devil," comes a low rumble from the doorway. Everett leans against the door frame of the kitchen. "Ains, there's a small cache in the closet of the guest room down the hall."

"Got anything good?" she asks, raising an eyebrow. "Boss tends to give you the latest and greatest."

"Go see for yourself," says Everett. She gleefully skips down the hall.

I try not to look at Everett, try not to exude anything that feels like pressure.

"What's the message?" he asks.

"We have to take the laptop to a helipad tonight. I have to go with it to unlock it."

He looks around the kitchen and nods. "Ainsley said I shouldn't come?"

"Yeah. How do you feel?"

He leans back against the counter across from me and dips his head side to side. "Not great. I don't think I could hold a gun properly. I can kind of shoot one-handed, but it's shaky. Haven't practiced it in a while."

He opens the fridge and stares into it, using his good hand to shuffle through what's there.

"I wish I could cook," he mutters.

I close the laptop with a snap and go back to picking at my cuticles. If he called, he would tell me, right? He said he would, but he didn't say when.

"I haven't called," says Everett.

I might love him to death and want to be respectful, but time is of the essence. "And how many times has Mr. Delancey called?" I ask.

"I wouldn't be surprised if he just showed up here."

He finally turns to look at me and we're both staring

daggers at each other. Eventually, I shrug my shoulders in surrender, despite my impatience.

I try to calm myself by putting myself in his shoes. It starts with the truth that there are some parts of his life that I will never understand. I will never know what it's like to realize your adoptive parents are involved in the world of crime. I can't even imagine an equivalent for me. Maybe like if I found out my mom's charity foundation was a front for funneling money to terrorists or something. If I found that out...

Ouch.

I square my shoulders. "I'm going to tell Mr. Delancey something that basically says that we've grown so close over all our years of working together that we fell in love and felt it best to marry in secret so as not to distract from the work of Milenna and the Beauty Done Well Initiative."

Everett shakes his head. "Love? That's not going to go well when we file the divorce papers."

My eyes go wide.

"Who said anything about divorce papers?" I ask sharply.

"Well, it's a marriage of convenience, Laina. Once the convenience ends, so does the marriage."

"We are not on the same page about that," I say, my tone and expression as serious as I can make them.

Everett's phone buzzes with a text notification and he reads it to himself, then blows out a breath. "Mr. Delancey says if you don't answer him, he'll come up with a statement himself."

"No, we're talking about this. About us, now. I'm not putting this off any longer."

"What are you saying?" Everett asks, slowly, with curiosity.

I don't want to just blurt it out to him right here in the

kitchen. I want mood lighting and my hand on his face and a searing kiss and a night to ourselves to unpack everything that we've been keeping pent up.

Everett denies yet another call while I map the planes of his cheekbones and sharp jaw line, his smooth skin and dark eyebrows, trying to memorize everything about him.

"You're so handsome," I say, starting softly, trying to work up the nerve to be brave. "I've always thought that about you. That you're the most handsome man in my life. But I was your boss, so it would have been a little forward to say it."

His eyes trace over my face. "You are so beautiful," he murmurs. "If you're allowed to say it, so am I." He's smiling, but his right hand is in motion, his fingers counting against his thumb. One, two, three, four. Four, three, two, one.

"What are you worried about?" I ask.

He laughs. "What am I not worried about?"

"You should come sit down." I wait for him to come over and take a seat on the barstool next to me. Everett's expression is guarded and fear gets the best of me. What if I ruin it all? What if I've misread everything up to this point? I can't jump in the deep end yet.

"What are you most excited about at your next posting?"

He takes a second to answer. "I guess I can travel a bit, see some places I haven't been to yet."

"Is it really going to be good for your career?"

"Yeah, it's more on the diplomatic protection side, working with people who negotiate different agreements and do international mediation. The more experience I gain, the higher I can set my contract prices. But that's not why I'm doing it."

What are his contract prices? How does he get paid? I

want to know everything about him, about every little way his mind works, about his job, what drives him. I want to know about everything he wants in life. I need more time with him, but it's as elusive as sand dropping down the hourglass.

"What's the end goal? To make more money?"

He shakes his head. "No, not just that. More like, peace, financial security. Be able to provide for a family, some kids. Make enough to retire at an age where I can still enjoy life."

"Do you get scared?"

"Sometimes, especially when it's personal. You know, you're my first close protection assignment ever. Normally, I'm running logistics for political summits and high-profile events, which is much more my thing."

I smile, thrilled that I'm special and unique for that reason. "Why did you take my assignment?"

"Boss—his name is Gideon, but we just call him Boss—he noticed I was in a slump at work. I felt unfulfilled and useless. I was probably a little depressed. Then out of nowhere, Boss told me the agency got assigned a short-notice contract and he needed me to fill it, didn't really give me a choice. I flew up from D.C. and met you in the living room like twelve hours later."

My eyes fill with tears as my heart swells with growing courage. "I remember the first minutes of that hour, when no one else would look at me except you. And you made me spaghetti that night."

He nods. "That first time I saw you, you looked right at me and even in that awful moment you were so beautiful. And then we started working together, finding our rhythm, and you weren't uptight or prissy. You listened to me. You acknowledged me. You were everything I had been missing. Still are."

We smile at each other with sadness and nostalgia, but the longer we look into each other's eyes, the more the feelings I have for him grow and expand until I feel like I can't breathe because of how much I love him.

How do we go on from this? How do we go from sharing such deep memories with one another, from living a fast-paced, slightly traumatic lifestyle together to not being in each others' lives anymore? How do we stop doing this, stop igniting fires with our eyes when we look at each other? How am I supposed to give that up?

I take his hand and lace my fingers through his and study the way we fit together like two halves of a whole.

"Why would you decide to leave me?" I ask, finally ready to know the truth.

Everett takes a shaky breath, clinging to my hand for dear life. "You are the most amazing woman I've ever met. You're beautiful and smart and you're driven, motivated. You know what you want and you go after it, but you're also kind and caring. You make me excited to wake up every day, just to see how you see the world, to hear the thoughts you have. I love being your friend. But I'll always, always want to be more than your friend. I love you. My heart is yours, Laina Milenna."

I gasp, my eyes flying to his.

"You never...I never thought—" I say, looking for the right words to respond with but coming up with nothing logical.

I never thought being loved in return was an option. My heart is beating a rhythm of ecstasy, making it hard to think. I knew there were feelings, interest, desire. There was genuine care and definitely chemistry. But love? I didn't dare wish for love.

He smiles sheepishly. "I'm the poster boy for being stupidly in love. Every morning, I would start with the hope that maybe one day you would look at me differently too. And every night, I would go to bed with frustration and disappointment. I wondered if you would ever feel the way I did and the more time passed, the more it became clear that I would be nothing more to you than your bodyguard and sure, a form of a friend. I was hurting, every day. So I made the impossible choice to move on, request a new assignment."

"Everett," I exhale and I'm smiling wider than I ever have in my life, looking into his gorgeous dark eyes. I want to laugh, I want to cry. Why couldn't we have figured all this out sooner?

"Why are you laughing?" he says, with a stormy frown.

I take his face in my hands. "Because I never, ever want to be just your friend, Everett Park. I want so much more."

His eyes widen. "Don't say that just because I said it."

"I'm not, I promise. I care about nothing and no one more than I care about you." I pull his hand to my lips and kiss it. He stands up, tall and looming over me and I wrap my arms around his waist. Sitting on the barstool puts me at the perfect height to rest my head near his heart. I close my eyes, soaking in the sound of his heartbeat, the rise and fall of his chest, the way his hand wraps around my head and presses me to him.

"I want this forever. I never want to let you go," I say softly, pressing a kiss to his chest. I'm content to listen to the rapid thump of his heart.

I hear a dial tone. My eyes fly open. The sight of Everett

looking down at me with a small smile makes me weak as love surges through every vein. He's holding his phone on speaker between us and the caller ID says he's calling a lawyer's office. He drops a kiss to my hair as we wait for them to pick up.

"Offices of Livel and Voeller."

Everett introduces himself and explains why he's calling. They place him on hold and I squeeze my arms around his waist, hugging him tight.

"Mr. Park, Matt Voeller," says a new voice through the phone.

Mr. Delancey calls again and Everett brushes the notification away.

"Yeah, hi," says Everett. "I am calling in regards to my parents' will, Adam and Beth Lourden. I believe your office has tried to get in contact with me, but uh, I've never had the opportunity to review their will and estate after their death."

There's a pause. "Yeah, let me pull that up. Would you like to come in to the office and we can go over that?"

"I'm afraid that's not possible at the moment. Not to be crass, but there's really only one provision that I'm interested in at the moment, purely for legal reasons. Are you the executor?"

"Yes, is there something specific you're interested in?"

"Is there anything that happens once I marry?"

There's a long pause and I don't breathe for any part of it. Everett dips his elbow down to poke at my arm, trying to loosen my hug. I hadn't realized I've been squeezing the breath out of him.

"Okay, here we go, just got to that section."

I might throw up. I pray and hope and wish and cross my fingers and manifest every good thing for Everett, my guy.

"Yep, yeah, it looks like your parents left you quite a bit, and there's a specific property you get once you marry, a little estate and farm in New Hampshire."

I stand on the footrest and throw my arms around Everett's neck, kissing his cheek, my heart pounding like fireworks of celebration. I'm too happy to cry. I want to do a dance, but Everett's standing there in stunned silence.

"But there's a lot more than that. You inherit basically everything they had, with the exception of some sizable charitable donations."

"Okay, thank you for letting me know," Everett says, his voice strained and emotional.

"There are also some letters, I think..." His voice trails off, as if looking for something, then comes back on the line, "We'd like to execute this as soon as possible, when would work for you?"

"Um..." Everett's not crying, but I can tell it's all hitting him like a ton of bricks. "I'll need to get back to you to set that up."

"Okay, just give us a call when you have a specific date in mind, and we'll make sure we accommodate you."

"Thanks so much," says Everett. The lawyer ends the phone call with a pleasantry and Everett sets his phone on the counter, looking absolutely stunned.

I can't hold back a giggle, even though I know it's entirely inappropriate.

"What?" he says gruffly.

"You own a farm," I say, gripping his good arm and giving him a little shake. "You, Mr. Hot Big City Bodyguard, you own a farm."

I get that he's going to need time to process this. I don't

want him to feel pressured to be happy. But I can't hold back that I'm ecstatic for him. I hope this is the first step in a long road of healing, of getting what he needs in order to reconcile his memory of his parents.

"What if it's all bought with blood money?" he asks.

"Or what if the blood money is the amounts they set aside for charities?" I counter.

He nods. "I'll have to find out before I feel anything close to relief."

"Of course," I murmur. He looks down at me and I grin at the glimmer of hope I see in his expression.

Mr. Delancey calls again and I know I have to take it this time. Everett passes the phone to me and my hand brushes his. What is it about a gentle hand brush that sets my skin on fire? I can press my whole body to him with calmness and comfort, but the minute there's a whisper of a touch, I have millions of butterflies in my stomach and my face is flaming.

"You should take that," says Everett, pressing another kiss to my hair. "Whatever you say, I'll be okay with," he promises. "I'm going to go rest on the couch."

I nod and he leaves me alone in the kitchen.

I answer the phone with confidence, not letting Mr. Delancey get the first word in. "I have it."

CHAPTER 16

I DIG through my chaotic closet and pull on a black mock turtleneck, black leggings, and find my black baseball cap in my messy hat drawer. With a black coat, I'll be ready to blend in with the night. I slip into some black Doc Martens and start to feel the power of an all-black outfit.

"Laina!" I hear Ainsley shout from somewhere down the hall.

"Just a minute!" I yell back.

I'm about to leave my closet when Everett comes in and immediately closes the door behind him, trapping us inside the small, dark space. I stand still, waiting for his next move. He must have been to his room and refreshed his cologne because warm tones of citrus are swirling in the air.

"Hi," I whisper for some reason, my heart rate jumping through the roof as he slowly walks towards me. "Have you seen it?"

The statement to the board should have gone out by now and I agreed with Mr. Delancey that it was okay to leak it to the press. I hope I've said the right thing.

"I have," he whispers back. He pulls out his phone and the light of the screen illuminates his face. I can't tell what sort of expression he has. "Want me to read it?"

"Yes, please."

He clears his throat and reads in a voice that would make the top newscasters tremble for their jobs.

"The news of my marriage to Everett Park has been made public against our wishes. We always intended for our relationship to remain private, in the hopes that it would not detract from the greater goals and purposes we have as individuals.

Everett Park is independently wealthy and received an additional inheritance as a result of our marriage, nullifying any motive to take advantage of my financial situation. To those questioning my judgment, I would say that the consideration and maturity I put into the decisions regarding The Milenna Company follow me into my private life. If choices made in private preclude one from leadership, then most of the board would be disqualified as well.

As to the state my husband and I were in when news broke of our marriage, we were victims of a home invasion. Thanks to Everett's training and intuition, I was kept safe. However, Everett sustained an injury to his shoulder which required surgery. The police are actively involved in the case and my husband is healing without complication.

You can expect to see me back in the office soon, there is work to be done."

I hold my breath, waiting to see what Everett says next. Hearing it read back, does it sound a little preachy, a little stuffy, a little like a speech made by a royal palace in England or something?

"Is it too...I don't know...bossy?" I ask.

"It's you, it's your voice," says Everett. If I'm not mistaken, I think he's a little proud of me and that thought makes me thrilled beyond belief.

"I just wanted it to be as true as possible. I hope it works in our favor. Mr. Delancey said it would help."

Everett nods, scrolling down his screen with a grin.

"What?"

"'Our wishes', 'my husband.'"

He shakes his head, locking his phone and sliding it into his pocket, plunging us into darkness before I can read his expression. He puts his good arm around my waist and pulls me towards him, holding me like I'm precious, of value. I have no objections, I melt into him. He rests his forehead on mine.

"Listen to me, I love you and I want you to be safe, understand? It's okay to be scared, all that matters is that you stay safe. Come back to me."

I nod against his head, closing my eyes to better hear the way our breaths match each other in frequency.

"It'll be okay," he promises.

He moves his hand to swoop around the back of my neck and into my hair, pressing into me, his cheek next to mine. My heart falls for him a million times over. I move my hands to either side of his face and as much as I want to devour him and kiss him senseless, I whisper to him instead. "I love you so much. For days on end, I've had my heart broken by wanting you and believing you could never be mine. You are the most incredible man in the world. I want you, only you, always."

He shivers and my knees go weak as I wrap my arms around his neck and hug him as gentle-tight as I can.

Everett's arm is back around my waist and my hands settle on his broad chest. I can feel his heart pounding away. I don't know who's more scared, but I know we need the press of our bodies together for reassurance.

I lift my chin and this is it, the moment where all it would take is him bending his neck a few degrees and I could kiss him. Everything in me is begging to kiss him, for him to kiss me, for us to fully dive in.

I hear Ainsley call for me again. Everett backs away from me and I already miss the warmth and power of his body. The absence of his pulse under my hands and the loss of his breath in my ear is awful. I don't know how to move on from this when I want to live in this moment for so much longer.

"See you soon," I murmur with one last touch of my hand to his face. "Love you, Ev."

I quickly walk out the closet door, steeling my resolve, only to have a strong hand grab my upper arm and pull me back into the closet. Everett pushes me up against the wall, kicks the door closed, and presses his mouth to mine. First one long, force of a kiss followed by slower, but equally passionate sweeps of his full lips.

My hands drift to his waist where I grab his sweatshirt in my fists, pulling him to me. He breaks the kiss, only to come back for more, but this time interjecting each kiss with a whisper.

"Do you know," soft kiss to my temple, "how long," a kiss to my throat, making me feel I've left reality and entered a fantasy, "I have waited and wanted to hear," another kiss up my neck, "that exact sequence of words," a kiss just to the right of my mouth.

I find the curve of his ear with my lips as I tangle my fingers in his hair and whisper. "Love you, Ev. I love you."

He claims my mouth as his again and I am eager for more.

More of this, every day, this and only this. To say I love you constantly, to kiss with wild abandon, to feel my heart burst and my head spin, to do every hot thing that's running through my mind right now with Everett and Everett only.

I run my hands over the soft velvet of his short hair at the base of his head and around his smooth jaw to hold his face, not letting him back away from this kiss. Let Ainsley wait, let her walk in on us, I don't care, I want this forever. It's solidifying that, all this time, Everett has not only been a friend but a soulmate. He is my other half, my love.

Everett draws back, taking a ragged breath that ends in a little laugh.

"What?" I whisper.

"I don't believe this is happening," he whispers back, his forehead against mine. "You're here and you love me and you're kissing me."

I smile and nod against him. As much as I want to stay in this moment forever, I know the clock is ticking on our mission. Now I just want it done and out of the way so I can hurry back to exploring this, this new dream come true.

I press my face into the crook of his neck and take a breath of air that smells blessedly like Everett. I am now intimately acquainted with the scent of his skin—clean, warm, and with a hint of his cologne—and it's intoxicating.

"Officially obsessed with you," I tell him, pressing a quick kiss to the underside of his jaw.

He hums in agreement, wrapping his arm around my shoulders and hugging me to his chest. "I love you, Laina." He sneaks in another kiss.

"Hey, stop making out with your hot bodyguard and get out here," Ainsley shouts through the closet doors, so close I jump. Everett laughs in triumph, a sexy, low rumble, and I can't keep a grin off my face.

I come out into the hallway first, shoving the baseball cap on my head and hoping it hides how many times Everett pushed his fingers through my hair. Everett's a few paces behind me, completely unabashed that his lips are red and swollen.

I did that.

"Ainsley," he says, his voice rough. "You guard her with your life. You don't let anyone lay a hand on her. Watch your back and always make the safest choice possible."

"Don't worry, I got you," she says with a nod, slipping a gun into a shoulder holster and grabbing the keys.

"See you soon, Ev," I say, winking at him as he smolders at me and gives me a farewell salute.

"Gross," Ainsley sighs as we head to the back door. "Way to kill my crush."

CHAPTER 17

WE DRIVE out of our underground garage, Ainsley at the wheel, me checking out a little taser that Ainsley found in Everett's closet. The night air is freezing, even in the car, and there's a glistening of snow melting as soon as it hits the road. Ainsley starts to list out instructions.

"When we get there, if you hear a drone, that's probably my tech guy back at Black Swan who's going to provide over-watch for us. We can't validate the security of the message that got sent, and although you're the only who knows the code phrase, we're expecting bad company at the drop. Obviously, the Vidovic Group would love to nab this, but there are other groups that would benefit from using it as leverage. Everyone's going to be sending their top mercenaries out."

Ainsley fishes around in the pocket of her coat and puts a little earpiece in her ear. I watch her in awe. I tuck the taser in my pocket and pop the collar of my wool coat to add to the aesthetic, but I'll never be as cool as Ainsley.

"You're like a super badass security girl," I tell her, "but you're also a really good assistant."

Ainsley smiles. "I probably have to work twice as hard as someone who's actually trained for that kind of stuff, but I'm glad you never had any issues. And truth be told, Boss kind of overreacted about Everett's obsession with you. If anything, Everett's extra protective of you."

Right, Ainsley was just there to cover for Everett. But what if he's not there anymore?

"Are you going to stay on now that Everett's leaving?"

Ainsley hesitates, waiting until she completes a left-hand turn to answer.

"Well, I've been thinking about that."

I wince. It's definitely not the exuberant and affirmative "Yes, of course!" that I wanted her to say. So I lose Ainsley too?

"What can I do to convince you to stay?" I ask. "The world is going to look a lot different once my dad comes back and we can reshuffle leadership and responsibilities. Even if you want to try something different, not necessarily being my assistant, like having your own position if there's a department that interests you, that'd be cool."

Ainsley is quiet, focusing on driving through a mess of taxis, Ubers, and pedestrians.

"And of course, you totally deserve a raise."

She keeps checking her rear and side view mirrors.

"I would just hate to lose you at Milenna."

She hums something and I can't tell if it's a murmur of agreement or not.

"Everything okay?"

"Yeah," she finally says. "In New York it's so hard to tell if you have a tail or not since all the cars are basically the same black town car or yellow taxi."

"You think we're being followed?" I go on the alert,

turning in my seat to scan the cars to the sides and behind us. There are a lot of blacked-out windows.

"Maybe. Don't worry, I'm the agency's best defensive driver. Just sit back and we'll get there fine."

I face forward again and let Ainsley do her thing.

"There's something I do need to talk to you about," she says, eyes glued to the road. She takes a minute to search for a few choice words. "Okay, well let me just put this out there." She starts to make some vague gestures with her hand as she navigates multiple lanes of traffic. "Uh, in most high-profile cases against criminal organizations, evidence is not enough. Witnesses are required and of course, they are putting themselves in extreme danger in order to testify or do a deposition or whatever. Law is not my strong suit. Anyways, they're in danger for doing that, so much so that it's usually in their best interest to enter a witness protection program."

I'm following what she's saying, but my brain can't apply it yet. What does that matter to me?

"And most people we know would take the option that's in their best interest. The option that keeps them alive. Especially if there's already been an attempt on their life."

My jaw drops as the full weight of what she's alluding to hits me square in the chest, knocking the breath out of me.

"You're saying my dad—"

"No, no, no," Ainsley waves her hands in front of her in a desperate attempt to cut me off. "I'm not saying anything about anyone, I'm just giving you some information about criminal cases." She widens her eyes at me as if to say *Don't say anything else.*

"I'm just saying that in my experience, witnesses never

return to their former lives. And I don't expect this to be any different."

It's like someone kicked me in the stomach.

"But–" I try to pick out words that won't be too specific. "Usually, they inform their families of that in some way, right?"

Ainsley shakes her head. "Not usually."

I feel sick. "No, he let me believe...look, I understand being safe and witness protection and all that. But that means I've been lied to."

"Honestly, Laina, anyone can let you believe what you want if it benefits them in some way."

Have I been blindsided by my own father? My chest goes tight as I cycle through disbelief and hurt. I don't know who I'm more upset at, Ainsley for correcting me or my dad for pulling the ultimate bait-and-switch.

"I should have known this sooner," I whisper, my voice shaking with anger.

"I honestly thought you did until just now."

A surge of violence rolls through me and I want to hit something, a feeling I've never experienced before.

Was I stupid, naive? Or did my dad want me to believe that he'd come back so I would be motivated to access the dossier? Am I truly never going to see him again?

Honestly, what the hell?

I seethe in silence the rest of the drive as reality continues to hit me in cold bursts. I am the CEO of Milenna and no one is coming to change that. It's me, the last Milenna, because my father will probably have to change his name. I hate it, I hate it all. I hate the hope that was snatched from me, the peace I thought I could have. Why did I think that this would just be the magical problem solver and everything would be so wonderful after this?

Ainsley doesn't say anything else to me, but she does talk through her earpiece to someone named Scotty about the drone and flight paths along the Hudson River. She's giving more attention to the rearview mirror.

"Get off my line, Evvy," she shouts as we start weaving through traffic. "We have a tail."

Good, I hope we're being followed. I hope I get terribly hurt, not killed, but terribly hurt and my dad has to live with himself for the rest of his life knowing that my mom died and I'm maimed for life and it's all his fault.

Okay, that was a thought too far.

"We good?" I ask Ainsley.

"I don't think so," she mutters. "Grab the laptop."

I pick it up from where it's been sitting at my feet the whole car ride.

"When I throw the car across the pier, run it to the helo while I cover for you." Ainsley's tone is suddenly serious as she pivots to watch behind her and look in front of us.

We're on a street that stretches down to the water for half a mile and ends in a straight shot to a pier with a helipad at the end. The helipad is empty.

"I need to know you heard me," Ainsley says.

"Got it," I reply.

Ainsley grins, a glimmer of danger in her eyes.

"You ready for this? Brace yourself for the drift."

I hug the laptop to my chest and plant my boots firmly on the floor of the car. She accelerates towards the pier, almost catching air as we hit the top of the last downhill at high speed. She hits the gas, cranks the wheel left, yanks the hand brake and we skid to a perfect stop, perpendicular to the pier.

I click out of my seatbelt and hesitate. There's still no helicopter. I should wait until I at least hear the steady thump of its propeller approaching.

Bullets hit the car, shattering the glass in all the windows. Ainsley and I instinctively duck and protect our heads as shards rain down over us.

"That's not supposed to happen!" Ainsley shouts.

She shoves me out the passenger side and dives out behind me, rolling to her left to use the front of the car as a barrier.

"Go!" she yells.

I take off racing down the pier towards the helipad, not realizing it's a bit of a mirage and there's more distance to cover than I predicted. I'm glad I'm still in decent running shape. I shift the laptop to my left arm and pump my right arm as I go full speed. The pier goes quiet behind me, no more gunshots ring out, and I hope that's a good thing.

Just as I'm wondering why I chose boots instead of running shoes, a tall black figure hauls itself up and over the side of the pier, dripping wet and covered in neoprene. It rises, menacing, and runs for me.

I scream in terror. I know it's probably some kind of mercenary, but I can't even see a face. They're like a specter of evil. But in my horror, I don't realize that I've kept right on running towards them.

"Take this!" I shout and throw the laptop down the pier, hoping they either go for it or I can barrel my way past them.

Both hopeful efforts are an epic fail.

I smash into the person, who I can now tell is a woman, with my elbows out, but she manages to keep herself from getting the wind knocked out of her. She grabs straight for my neck, which I was not anticipating, and gets her hand around my throat in an iron grip. She manages to dance around my feet as I kick and claw at her hands, gasping for breath.

She has height on her side and I'm realizing that she wants me to pass out, but she's in no rush. Her lack of urgency is terrifying. She squeezes harder and reaches under my coat and around my back, somehow intuiting that's where I've strapped the actual laptop. A fiery ache fills my throat and my body starts going limp before I'm ready.

Is this how I go? Choked to death on a fool's errand to get my dad back? Without saying goodbye to Everett, cheated of a future with the love of my life?

No. No, this is not it.

Anger surges and my fight reflex kicks back in. I don't stop flailing my limbs and trying to land a hit. I want to hurt someone. It's a dark feeling, one I don't want to encourage in my normal life, but for now, it could be the difference between life and death. I take my hands off hers and claw at her face. I manage to get her focus off the laptop and then I remember.

I've been an idiot this whole time.

I manage to fish the taser out of my pocket and with all my might, I suddenly swing my legs and throw my weight, pushing into her, getting her off balance. I point the taser at her and fire away, hoping that some shock made it through her neoprene suit, at least enough to get this laptop away and me safely back in the car.

Miraculously, she lets go of me, slumping into a black pile on the pier.

I drop the taser with its leads still in her and keep heading for the helipad. There's still not the faintest sign of an inbound aircraft, but there are more mercenaries crawling up out of the water. I stop just shy of the "H" marked in a circle as four of them stalk towards me, dripping wet. I chance a glance over my shoulder and can just see Ainsley in the light from a nearby lamppost, crouching behind the shot-up car, reloading her pistol.

A fresh wave of fear rushes through me and I shiver in the frigid air. This feels like an ambush. There might not even be a helicopter coming. Someone could have hacked that whole secret messaging system and lured us here. This feels like a total mistake.

There are two choices and it's up to me to decide. I can trust that I'll be able to hand this laptop over soon or I can run back towards Ainsley and we try to get out of here. I don't have a radio. Ainsley's still holding her end of the pier. Everett's at home. No one is going to decide for me or come make this better. I'm on my own. I have to make my own way forward.

I can do this. I haven't studied martial arts since sixth grade, but thanks to adrenaline I'm mildly confident this is going to work out.

I take a boxing stance, planting my feet and raising my fists, and wait for the first all-black mercenary to charge me. A blast of freezing cold air and a hint of sleet whips across my face, causing me to squint my eyes. I try to anticipate which of the four figures are most likely to be the one that injures or kills me. I decide to go down swinging at the shortest one and just as I lunge towards them, there's a rapid popping sound and all of them suddenly crumple to the ground.

The icy wind picks up faster and faster and I hold my hand up trying to brace against it. A massive dark shape drops down onto the helipad, then lights come on. It was never wind, it was all air being pushed away from this black, soundless helicopter.

A door on the side slides open and a man in a dark suit and black-framed glasses steps out. He undoes his jacket and pulls a handgun out of his shoulder holster, aiming it just to my right.

"Come on!" he shouts.

The rotors are still spinning and I shield my face with my arm to try to get enough space to breathe as I approach him.

"What's the passphrase?" the guy yells.

"It's snowing in the Black Hills!" I shout, then wince in pain. My throat feels like someone ran a sander over it, then hit it with a mallet.

He nods and plugs a device into a phone, setting it on the seat of the helicopter. "I'll cover you. Put in the prints and get out of here."

I drop my coat and unwind the ace bandages Ainsley wrapped around me, grab the laptop from behind my back, and set it down next to the device, ready to scan my fingerprints the moment the screen lights up.

Out of curiosity and concern for Ainsley, I make the mistake of looking over my shoulder. The pier is still crawling with mercenaries. There must have been at least a dozen more that have emerged.

"Focus!" shouts the guy and I shoot him a scathing glance. I get the fingerprints in and watch the screen unlock, then flood with files.

"Can I check the contents?" I ask him, shouting through the pain of my injured throat.

"Of course not!" he barks back.

I steel myself to raise my voice over the noise of the rotors.

"I need to see what Adam Lourden put on there." I want this for Everett, for him to have closure that his dad did the right thing in the end.

"No way," says the guy. He slides the laptop over, shoves me out of the way, and is about to slide the door closed, but I grab it and pull back, fury fueling me with unnatural strength.

"What about my dad, what about Henry?"

The guy shakes his head. "Henry Milenna is dead to you."

He slams the door shut and I have enough common sense to rapidly get off the helipad.

Ainsley is making her way towards me and I run towards her, angry yet relieved, upset but content. When the final answer is the final answer, that's what you have to live with.

Everything is noise and chaos as Ainsley shouts into her earpiece and fires her gun at the same time. I crouch down next to her.

"We still need to get out of here," she says. "I bet some of these guys would love to take you hostage. We're pretty pinned down though and the car is totaled. I mixed up the cars like an idiot and left the bulletproof one at the house."

"What do we do?" I ask. "We can go over the side and swim home."

"It's too cold," she shouts back.

"We can't just wait here! Let's climb to the underside and we can walk across the trusses or hang from them like monkey bars."

Ainsley shakes her head and looks around the pier. "I'll figure something out. Last resort, Scotty will call the cops."

"I can't have my name in the news again," I shout as Ainsley fires off another round.

"That's why I said last resort."

There's a momentary flash of light coming down the road that leads to the pier, like headlights going over a speed bump. All the shooting dies down for a moment and I hear a deep, distinct revving of an engine. The car flies towards the pier and doesn't hesitate for a second. It smashes straight into our car now pockmarked with bullets, shoves it to the side, and speeds towards us.

"We should run," says Ainsley, frozen in place.

I hesitate for half a second, then my body almost melts into the pier with relief. I know that car.

"It's Everett."

He can't shoot a gun one-handed, but he's driving the hell out of the bulletproof car. He swings wide and across the pier in a squeal of tires and cloud of burning rubber. The window rolls down and there sits my husband with a look of pure fire in his eyes.

"Get in," he roars over the dull thunk of bullets hitting the car.

I go straight for the front seat and Ainsley dives into the back seat. Everett takes off as soon as the doors close and the window's up.

"You're driving a stick shift with one hand!" Ainsley exclaims.

"Yes, and?" Everett retorts. His left arm is still firmly held in place by his sling and when he shifts gears, there's no control of the steering wheel.

"Oh my gosh!" I squeal, closing my eyes and bracing myself as Everett speeds down the pier and up the road, barely swings the whole car past incoming traffic, cutting off a cab who lays on the horn. I swear I can see the person in the back of the cab, their eyes big as saucers as we slide by. But somehow, we don't so much as scrape them.

"Is this even legal?" Ainsley exclaims.

"Can we focus on getting home for now?" I add.

Everett's driving is confidently riding the fine line between sexy and scary and while I'm in awe, I'm also terrified we're going to crash. His eyes focus on the road and his jaw muscle ticks as he stays in the zone, shifting and weaving through the cars on the road like a racing professional.

"Trust me, we're going home," he says.

CHAPTER 18

Everett swings open the door from the garage to the house and I've never been so happy to see the familiar hallway lights. I stumble in behind Ainsley and Everett is already berating her.

"You almost got her killed," he says, his voice a growl. "You were overconfident and you messed up."

When our eyes connect, Everett rushes to me and pulls me close, tilting my chin up with one finger towards the light. My neck must be bruising and he looks furious about it. His eyebrows are drawing together in concern, his eyes pained.

"You were a useless distraction," Ainsley hisses at him. "You made yourself a liability, Everett. I am her agent right now, not you."

"I might not be point, but I'm going to be giving Boss a full incident report," he shoots back.

"What's going on?" I ask.

Ainsley crosses her arms and juts her chin towards Everett.

"He patched into the radio frequency that Scotty set up.

He was trying to keep tabs on you. But he kept jabbering in my ear and I could barely hear Scotty."

Affection and understanding for Everett flood my heart. If I could have hacked my way into the operating room speakers to listen to the surgeon while he stabilized Everett, I would have totally done it. I wrap my arms around his waist and hug him tight. He puts his arm around me and leans down to rest his chin on my head. His warmth is comforting.

"You let someone hurt my wife," says Everett in a husky, choked voice.

I've never heard a sentence so aggressively romantic. I'm done, I am hopelessly in love forever. This man, my guy.

"I'm okay," I say, holding my hands out for everyone to calm down. "It all went okay. We're back and we'll live and I don't even need surgery or a hospital stay."

He looks down at me and I raise an eyebrow at him, a subtle reminder that what I watched him go through was a lot worse than a few marks on my neck and a sore throat. He gives me a quick kiss of reassurance and I follow it up with one of my own, a reminder that we both just made it through situations that scared the other person.

"We did it. It's over," I remind him.

"Look, I messed up and I'm sorry for the mix-up, everyone," Ainsley says, quietly. "Truly, things would have gone a lot smoother if I hadn't done that."

I squeeze Everett's hand, gentle at first, then harder the second time.

"Fine," he grumbles. "It could have been worse."

"And I forgive you for your blind rage fueled by undying love. Laina, you did great. I'm going to find a spare room here and grab some sleep."

"We need to go in to Milenna tomorrow," I say quickly before she leaves. "All of us."

"We'll talk about it," says Everett.

"We'll talk about it," I repeat, giving him a look that says I'm not going to change my mind.

"Okay, goodnight," says Ainsley with a wave.

Once it's just the two of us, Everett, cups my cheek in his hand. "How are you?"

There's still so much going on inside my head that I have to process. I can't stay still, can't sit down yet.

"Come with me?"

Everett follows me to the bathroom that connects to my room. He leans back against the counter in front of one sink while I turn on the faucet on the other sink. I splash freezing water on my face and blindly reach for my face wash. Everett places it in my hand.

"Want to talk about it?" he asks as I lather up my face.

"I'm so freaking mad," I admit through my hands.

I'm processing the events in slow motion. I've never had anybody lay their hands on me that way. I've always been protected from that, a privilege of my life circumstances. I never had any fear of violence in my life.

But the victims of the Vidovic Group, they're real people who have had to live with that every day as their reality. So, if I helped them in any way, I'm glad that I went through with the mission. Even if it wasn't what I thought it would be. Even if I didn't get what I truly wanted.

This is the most hollow victory I've ever experienced.

I wash the suds off my face as the tears start to fall. I sniffle and realize there are no big sobs or wails, just the steady, quiet grief of continued loss. I don't know why I'm trying to disguise it from Everett. But I feel silly for having hoped for something that would never happen. I grab a hand towel off the counter and bury my face in it.

"There was a guy there, with the helicopter," I say, muffled. "I asked him to see what your dad put in the dossier. But he said no."

I wipe my tears on the towel and set it down, sniffling one last time. I look over at Everett. He's pinching the bridge of his nose like he's trying not to cry.

"And he said my dad—" Maybe I was wrong about no big sobs. I hiccup one away. "He was so insensitive. He just said, 'Henry Milenna is dead to you.' And I was so shocked and angry and—" I stop talking and brush at my cheeks.

Everett comes closer and pulls me into his good shoulder.

"I thought he would come back. I miss my dad, I thought he would come back," I explain, crying into his chest.

"Oh, Laina love," Everett whispers, holding me as I sob.

I can't believe my own dad would know that he would see me one last time in his life and he would barely even hug me. I should have begged him harder, held on to him longer, let him see how weak and scared I can be. If I would have handled it better, been more honest and vulnerable with him, maybe he would have tried to find another way. But he knew what he was doing, and he let me believe what I wanted.

"I feel so betrayed. Like me, his only child, his own daughter—I wasn't a good enough choice."

"No, no, don't go down that road. That's not true," Everett says. "This has everything to do with the lies he's told himself. It has nothing to do with you."

"Ainsley said he's going to go into witness protection. Isn't that so stupid?" I wail like a toddler.

"That's unbelievable," says Everett, and to emphasize it he adds, "What a weirdo."

I laugh at his word choice and it's a brief reprieve. Tonight, I have no desire to protect the memory of my dad and I've decided Everett's allowed to call my dad names. Because my dad is making this decision like a weirdo.

I take a step back from Everett when I sense his body starting to slump with fatigue. He has to sleep sitting up because of his shoulder, so we make our way to the den and I curl up on one side of the sectional while he props himself up on the other side. But I come over to him to say goodnight, smiling despite my heartache. I get to kiss him goodnight for the first time ever.

Everett locks eyes with me and smiles back. I'm so grateful for him. It's been too long since I've kissed him and judging by the way he keeps dropping his eyes to look at my lips, he's thinking the same.

"Thank you for rescuing us," I say.

"I'll always come for you," he murmurs back. "Now, about tomorr—" that makes me quickly lay my hand over his mouth.

"Do. Not. Talk. About. Tomorrow," I command. "Rest."

"We need to," he mumbles, his lips moving across my hand. Did he just kiss my palm? His smoldering expression tells me yes and it's just as potent as the searing kiss he gave me at our wedding.

"And we need to talk about us," he says, punctuating it by pressing my hand to his mouth, kissing me with each word.

"Ev, I'm so tired, you wouldn't be getting my best," I reply. And then I counterattack by holding his face in my hands and pressing a kiss to his lips, so short he can't kiss me back. That's never going to get old. "Tomorrow, we're going to go in to the office like we always do and then we're going to come home and then we can talk about it."

"Better idea," he says, using his good hand to grasp my chin and pull me back for a kiss. He's sneaky fast, leaving me wanting more. "Everyone knows we're married. We don't need to hide out here."

I nod and we both go in for a quick kiss that turns into a long kiss that makes my stomach flip. Everett backs away, only a breath's width.

"Laina Milenna, will you go out to dinner with me?"

"Everett Park, I would love to go to dinner with you."

I don't know how long we kiss for. I don't know how we don't injure Everett's shoulder more as we savor being together late into the night. But I do know that my heart fills to overflowing, that Everett is my anchor and my soulmate and my love. And he whispers words in my ear that echo the thoughts in my heart, that tell me he feels the same.

CHAPTER 19

Ainsley, Everett, and I walk into the Milenna offices together the next morning. The paparazzi is swarming, and even though he insisted on coming, Everett is sore with limited range of motion, so Ainsley acts as a casual backup.

Once we're on the main floor, I turn into a tornado rushing around the office, taking in congratulations, things that have fallen off the radar, and more than a few jealous looks from women in the office who always eyed Everett.

There are calls to be made to the board members, good will to restore, and in the back of my mind, I'm keeping a running list of things that I hate about this job that I'll want to change going forward. If I'm brave enough.

The best part of my day is knowing that at the end of it, Everett and I are going to get to go to dinner and do something as low stakes as ordering food at an Italian restaurant. When I clock out around six, I nearly collapse with relief.

Ainsley kindly agrees to act as our chauffeur for the night. Everett and I sit in the back seat and Ainsley yells at us to keep our hands to ourselves.

When we get to the restaurant, Everett holds the door for me and gives the hostess his name. While she gathers the menus, he takes my coat and scarf and hangs them on the rack by the door. Or tries to. It's hard to do one-handed.

We're led to a cozy crescent-shaped booth that curves around a table covered with a red and white checked table-cloth. A slowly melting candle is stuck in an old Chianti bottle and I am in love with the snug, candlelit mood.

We slide in and sit just far enough apart that I can lean on the table and look Everett in the eye with a smile.

"What?" he says with a grin.

"Are we really doing this?"

"Doing what?"

"Going on a date. In public."

"Our first date" he says, like it's no big deal. But when he reaches for his glass of water, there's a shake in his fingers.

If someone would have told me a week ago I would be on a date with Everett, I would have blushed and laughed it off. But here we are.

"How was work today?" he asks.

"Exhausting." I lean an elbow on the table and rest my head on my hand. "It was a lot of managing emotions and decisions and boundaries. Lots of questioning looks I had to push past. Mr. Delancey and I are still trying to thaw that last little bit of a Cold War we have going on, but I think he just needs some time. He's like an uncle to me and I know what I did must have stung a little bit."

He nods. We stare into each other's eyes for so long that we lapse into a silence that slowly turns somber. I know what we need to talk about, but that doesn't mean I'm prepared.

"Ev," I say, but then the waiter comes and I pause so he can take our orders. Once he's gone, taking our menus with him, Everett loosens the knot under his shirt collar and with one hand slowly undoes his tie. I thought him rolling up his shirt sleeves was hot, but this is...this is something else. Is he for real right now? The tail of his tie flicks down into his lap and he slowly rolls it up.

"Stop trying to seduce the restaurant," I whisper.

He smiles at me coyly and undoes his top button, showing me just where to direct my hands if I want them to dive under his collar and feel the smoothness of his neck and the tops of his shoulders. He adjusts his shirt side to side, just enough for me to see a familiar silver chain.

My first thought is, "This sexy man is all mine" and my second thought is a heart-squeezing, "He's wearing it."

I look down at my left hand where I still proudly wear my ring. After all, I made a statement and there was nothing in that statement to imply that once we were found out that I would be ending my marriage. So for all intents and purposes, we are a happily married couple in the honeymoon phase.

But that ring on my hand, that ring around his neck, they mean so much more to us. Because they're not well and truly symbols of promised love. Not yet.

Everett takes my hand and interlaces his fingers with mine.

"Here's the thing," he says. There's just enough allowance in that statement to give me hope. "I signed a two-year contract and I'm going to have to pay the value of it if I don't show up on the job. It's a massive boatload of money and the contract is non-transferable. So, I'm still leaving."

"I'll pay it," I reply.

"We're not going to do that, Laina." He kisses my hand, a conciliatory gesture. "I could pay it if I was ready to take on my parents' money. But it's not about getting out of the contract. I think we would benefit from dating and figuring us out without all the formality of being CEO and bodyguard. We should have fun, make more good memories, figure out what we want out of our jobs and our lives. There's no rush."

I nod, squeezing his hand in an effort to also squeeze down the rising lump in my throat. I know what he's saying makes sense. I do have a lot to figure out with my role at Milenna and I want him to feel free to pursue what's important to him. I just wish it wasn't so far away, for so long.

"But I don't ever want to divorce you. I love you, so that wouldn't make sense anyways."

I'm about to create a very steamy public display of affection in this little Italian restaurant, but Everett drops my hand and puts a finger to my lips to hold me back.

"Therefore—"

"How many conjunctive phrases do you have?" I ask impatiently.

"Therefore," he says with a smile. "What I propose is that we date long-distance and act like we are not married. I think we deserve the growth that comes from dating. I for one need to come to terms with the reality of being with you, instead of the fantasy version I've built up in my head."

"Oh, do tell me about the fantasy," I say in a low voice, running my finger down his jaw.

"We never argue, you always take my side, I always make the best possible decisions, and you are constantly in awe of my alpha male prowess."

I laugh out loud, earning myself a gorgeous grin from Everett.

"What else?" I ask, sensing there's more. Everett takes a sip of water and nods.

"If we're as good together as we think we are, then we have a second wedding. Because I want a do-over at proposing to you and a do-over of getting to kiss my bride." His eyes are flashing with excitement and, in my peripheral, I see his hand resting on the table, his fingers counting in pattern. "What do you think?"

I go through a very quick rainbow of emotions that I can sum up as being upset. Upset by how in love with him I am, that I am totally willing to go to the ends of my emotional earth for him. But also, two years of long distance? It must be written all over my face because Everett can barely contain his grin as he delivers his last line, a direct quote from *Mission Impossible*.

"I can see that you're very upset."

My eyes fly wide with mock rage and Everett, smart man that he is, dives in for a kiss before I can act on it. Do I love him? Yes. Do I want him? Mercy, yes. Is two years a very, very, very long time? Also yes.

"We'll just go day by day," he says in a gentle voice. "We have a lot to figure out. You have a lot to figure out too with work and life and balance and us just kissing and making out all the time—"

"Kissing is absolutely the best way to figure things out," I argue, playfully.

Everett smiles with a telling blush. "Look, we can see each other as much as we want to. This is where it pays to have fallen in love with a wealthy city girl with her own private jet."

"The carbon offsets I'll have to buy." I roll my eyes and squeeze his hand and he squeezes back.

Our food comes and we talk as we eat, about inane things that are less charged, like the agency he works for and next steps for me with leaning more into my mom's legacy, finally committing time to her opera foundation.

As we're scraping up the last bites of tiramisu and Everett's paid the bill, we look at each other and smile.

"We're doing this," I say, with an excited smile.

"I can't believe there's a 'we', an 'us'," Everett says, taking my chin in his hand and kissing me.

LATER THAT NIGHT, we finally finish *Mission Impossible III*, which is my favorite so far. We skipped *II* because Everett said I would ruin it by laughing too much. We're snuggled up on the leather sectional in the den as the credits roll. Everett wraps his arm around my neck, his biceps cradling my face, pulling me towards him in the crook of his right elbow. He presses his forehead to mine.

"Leaving you, actually walking away and getting on the plane, is going to be nearly impossible."

I lean back and run my hand over his cheek in reassurance. He looks positively tormented and I want to soothe that away.

"When I asked to be reassigned," he says. "I wanted nothing more than to run away from what was daily heartbreak. But I want you to know that I'm not running away from you now. I hope you know that."

"I do. And it'll be okay," I whisper, giving him a kiss of reassurance. "I have my own work to do too. I finally realized that no one is going to give me permission to make this job more sustainable for me. It's up to me to make it a job I'll love instead of just enduring something I inherited."

"And you'll call me at the end of each day and tell me all about it."

"I will." I wrap my arms around his neck and hug him tight, my cheek pressing against his head and my hands messing up the back of his hair.

"I love you," he whispers to me. "Hearing you say all that makes me excited for the future."

"I love you, Ev," I whisper back, gently pushing his hair off his forehead. "We have a great future ahead of us."

I ONLY HAVE a few more days before my husband leaves for another country, and I've holed up in my office because I'm a mess, equal parts sad and self-pitying. Everett and I have been a bit short with each other, stress and insecurities getting the best of us. Even though we've known each other for so long, dating throws us into new roles and we're both humans with emotions and selfishness. It's not all rainbows and butterflies.

Tara, my therapist, has proven to be invaluable, both in my new relationship with Everett and in the areas that I can share with her. It sucks that I have to carry the weight of my dad's betrayal between Everett and I, but I'm grateful for the people in my life that are helping me through the good and the bad. I'm learning to delegate more, let go of my iron grip on the company and relax a bit. It's good, but hard.

I'm in the middle of reviewing a pitch presentation at my desk when Ainsley and Everett rush in with unreadable expressions and close the door behind them.

"What is it?" I ask, wary and nervous.

Everett swipes the remote off my desk and turns on the flat screen TV on the opposite wall. The major news networks immediately come up, but Everett flips past them to the BBC. The headline is bold and runs the entire length of the screen.

"Major Arrests in Massive Undercover Operation Against The Vidovic Group."

"No," I whisper in disbelief, standing and bracing myself against my desk.

The anchorwoman goes on to list the atrocities committed by the criminal group and the names of some of the ranking members that were arrested across Europe, including Vanya Vidovic.

"You did that," Ainsley says in awe, then she gets more animated. "We did that! It worked! Should I get champagne?"

It's everything I had hoped for. Vanya Vidovic, the man responsible for the death of Mom and Everett's parents and atrocities against so many others, being cuffed and shoved into a police van. He'll have to answer to justice now. It'll go to trial, the anchorwoman says. I just hope it's enough to truly stop the Vidovic Group.

"I think I'll just get back to work," I say.

Everett mutes the TV and comes to my side. "You okay?"

Ainsley gives me a bittersweet smile as she leaves and closes the door behind her.

"It's a big deal," I whisper to him, working to process how complicated all this is. It's a good thing for everyone, but it's even more final that I'll never see my dad again.

"It's a good thing. Really good," I say, making an effort. "Just still raw, I think."

"Do you see those guys being locked up?" Everett squeezes

my shoulder. "They're done, finished. You did something that had a domino effect that will save lives. Literally, you saved people's lives. I hope you're genuinely proud of yourself, Laina."

I lean into him, wrapping my arm around his waist.

"Thank you for everything," I say. "I couldn't have done it without you."

I am going to be without him so soon though. It's just a matter of time and then I'll wake up and he won't be there and I'll walk into work and he won't be there and I'll wander into the kitchen late at night and he won't be there. I can't stop myself from softly crying.

Everett turns us so he can lean back against the desk and hold me. He presses his lips to my hair in a prolonged kiss.

"I'm sorry, I didn't think you would be sad. If Mr. Delancey finds out I made you cry again, he's going to get me banned from the building."

I can't help but laugh.

"I'm going to miss you so much," I say.

"Listen," he says, drawing back enough to look me in the eye. "We're doing a really brave thing. It's going to be hard, no way around it. But time will fly. And then one day we'll be old and sitting in rocking chairs in a quiet corner of the world and it'll feel like a blip in time that we were ever apart."

"You'll still like me enough?" I ask, sniffling.

"Of course. Always," he says with a laugh that rumbles through his chest. And I take it as a promise.

CHAPTER 20

Two years (minus six weeks) later...

I don't hear any exclamations. There's no announcement.

The door swings open, in walks Everett. He kicks the door closed behind him and stares at me, power personified, bridled energy in his dark suit.

I sit behind my desk in stunned silence, my hands frozen on the armrests of my chair.

"Hey, gorgeous," he says, his voice rough. "Surprise."

I launch myself out of my chair and take a running jump into his open arms. Plural. I cling to him with my legs wrapped around his waist, thanking myself for choosing wide-legged slacks today. I hug the breath out of him, thrilled to see him again.

Eventually, he taps my butt, signaling that he'd like to get some air in his lungs. I loosen my grip around his neck a bit but stay held in his arms.

"My guy," I say in his ear. "You're here."

The kiss that follows is the sweetest. Our reunion kisses

just keep getting better and better. Everett surprising me for the first time just makes it all the more special.

"Okay, I'm putting you down," he says, walking us over to my desk, where he sets me on the edge closest to him.

"You aren't supposed to be back for another six weeks," I remark, pulling on his lapels so I can hold him close enough to sniff his neck again. The way my muscles relax at the smell of his cologne is utterly ridiculous and totally real.

"I have many surprises for you," he says, kissing my neck. "Oh, you smell good. That is beautiful. I think this might be the one."

In a late-night round of truth-or-dare during one of our overnight reunions in Europe, Everett finally confessed that after years of sharing close personal space with me, he never liked my Chanel No. 5. I acted offended at first, but truth be told, I was ready for a change too. So I've been trying different perfumes each time we meet up. This one, a subtle jasmine and pear scent, was supposed to be debuted in six weeks' time.

Everett dips his head under my chin, nuzzling under my collar and humming with happiness.

"I only have one more meeting," I say, closing my eyes. "I'm clocking out at a very reasonable hour, then I'm yours."

"No, you don't," he says in a low voice, kissing the hollow of my throat.

I push back on his head, rustling his hair a bit. I get to mess up his hair if I want to and I take advantage of it. Often.

"Just one more meeting and then I'm off for the whole weekend."

"You're mine starting right now," he says with a sly grin, kissing my lips in a way that makes me forget what day it is.

"But I—" I suddenly realize what he means. "Ainsley canceled my meeting, didn't she?"

"Mmhmm," he says with a triumphant tone. "And Garth knows to leave you to me."

Thank goodness Ainsley decided to stay on a few more years as my assistant. She also moonlights as my bodyguard when Garth and his wife want to go see the grandkids. And when I have any events that will go after midnight, because Garth does not cope well with anything past 12 a.m.

Sneaky Ainsley didn't give me a hint of Everett's surprise. I'm impressed. "So, you have me all to yourself. Big plans?"

"Yup." He gives me one more short kiss, then steps back entirely.

He takes my hand and with quick, confident movements, we're out the door of my office, through the bullpen, in the elevator, making out, out of the elevator, up some stairs, and on the roof of the building, the new spring air blowing all around us.

And I spy a photographer. Instinct makes me pull on Everett's sleeve and point.

"That's for us, just for us," he says with a knowing smile.

He leads me by the hand and angles me so that the prettiest view of the city skyline is behind me. There's a blue sky that I haven't seen yet today and the sun on my skin feels like a promise of a warm and happy summer.

Everett undoes the jacket of his suit and reaches into his breast pocket. I swiftly realize what's happening and I couldn't be happier. The swell of love and emotions that follow tells me this is going to be one of the best moments of my life.

Everett goes down on one knee, quickly pushes his hair back in place, and then holds up a stunning engagement ring with three giant diamonds, one oval in the center flanked by two round, all set in gold. I gasp.

Never in my wildest dreams could I have come up with a scenario this breathtaking.

"Laina Milenna, my love, you are my greatest joy, my best friend, my biggest encourager, and my most prized relationship. I love you with all that I am, and while you will always be out of my league, nothing would make your former bodyguard happier than to officially be your husband. Will you marry me?"

"Yes, Everett," I say, smiling while crying. "Yes, of course."

"Will you marry me this weekend, at my farm?" he says with a laugh.

"I would love to," I say, throwing myself at him, kissing him with all the meaning and gratefulness one can convey in a kiss.

THE NEXT DAY, we drive along a wooded road, no other cars in sight. I'm actually a little surprised, given that though we tried to keep it clandestine we were spotted walking out the back door of Kleinfeld's carrying white and black garment bags. But Everett's slick driving skills got us through traffic without any tails.

I'm typing on my phone, working on what I'm going to say to him. I've had a running note of things I've saved up to tell him, but as I look over it, nothing feels right. It all reads like reminiscences on the past, not promises for the future.

"I have something else to tell you," says Everett, breaking through my thoughts. He's got his left hand casually draped over the top of the steering wheel and his right arm is leaning on the console between us. His fingers are counting. I reach over and squeeze his knee. He takes a deep breath and gives me a quick smile.

"I quit my job at Black Swan."

I gasp. My mouth forms a giant "O" and my eyes go wide.

"You quit your job?" I ask in a reverent whisper. He had six weeks to go and the thought of him signing a new contract was constantly in the back of my mind. Of course we've discussed him looking for a job in New York, but so far he hadn't settled on anything.

He nods, a genuine smile now plastered on his face.

"I know we didn't talk about it, but after having the time to process everything in the will and the letters..."

Not long before he left for Poland, he met with the executor of the will and found that not only was his inheritance sizable, there were also long letters from his mother and father waiting for him.

His parents each asked for his forgiveness, for the parts they played in assisting the Vidovic Group, for the ways they failed him as parents, for everything they missed out on by not coming after him when he left. It was a big deal and we spent a lot of time talking through it together. We're each on our own journey of figuring out how to think of our parents in memoriam.

This announcement about quitting is something new that he's working up to telling me, and I'm on the edge of my seat, fighting for patience as he slowly forms his next sentence. "I found something I'm actually really invested in, security-wise, something personal."

"That's great, I'm so proud of you. What is it?"

He starts to grin again, but his voice gets a little choked up as he tells me. "I am now one of the executive security officers for Lourden Luxuries. My team will handle all security and logistics for purchases, transactions, and exchanges."

"Everett!" I exclaim, my eyes wide in awe.

"Our main office is down the block—"

"And around the corner from Milenna!"

I squeal and grab his arm, shaking him with excitement. Could this day get any better? We're getting married for real, we're going to work downtown together, we're going to build a life together. Together, together, together.

He grins. "I was going to wait to tell you, but I knew how happy you were going to be and I just couldn't hold it in anymore."

"Ev," I say, completely laugh-crying. "This is the best."

"You're the best," he says with a wink.

He makes a left-hand turn and we head down a smaller road, still paved, but only wide enough for a single car.

"This is it."

I shiver with excitement as we turn again and then the car noses down a steep driveway and the view in front of us is incredible. Everett brakes so I can take it in.

A large white farmhouse with green shutters and a wrap-around porch sits right in the middle of my view. There's a wide expanse of grass and meadow all around, dotted with trees and a few outbuildings here and there.

"Welcome to my humble farm, Wife," says Everett.

It's the perfect place for us, both rich in imagery and in meaning. It's my dream come true.

After we get our things settled in the master suite that will double as our honeymoon suite, I use a guest room to take a moment to myself and change into my wedding dress.

It's an ethereal white gown with billowing, gauzy sleeves and a deep V in the back. I saw it on display the minute we stepped into the store and knew it was the one, especially when it didn't require any alterations. I reverently step into it and, because of the low back, I'm able to zip it up myself. I pin my hair up in gentle twists to make a loose chignon and put in the pearl and gold chandelier earrings I picked out of the safe this morning, the same ones Mom wore on her wedding day.

I miss her the most. Getting involved in her foundation just revealed more and more of her true beauty of character, love for others, and passion for the arts. There were times where I had to excuse myself from conversations effused with her praise to go dry my eyes in the women's restroom. I wish she was here.

And I know I should long for my dad to be able to witness this, but I don't. I don't long for him at all. If he hears of my marriage and is heartbroken that he's missing his only daughter's wedding, well, that's what he gets for lying to me.

I don't necessarily blame him for it, I'm glad he's safe and hidden, but I do carry resentment. Maybe one day I'll work through that. Hard choices were made, and he is not here. I don't really wish it differently.

In fact, the only people I might have wanted with me are Ainsley and Mr. Delancey. But Everett and I decided that this was just for us. Our personal life as a new family begins today.

We're going to be Everett and Laina Milenna-Park.

I tuck the comb of the elbow-length veil into my hair and look over myself one more time. The last step is to slip my written vows into my capacious pockets and walk out to where Everett is waiting for me on the wide lawn, his back to me.

He's in a sharp black tuxedo, one of my favorite looks for him. I've seen him in a tux before, at a gala we went to together in London, but this time he's dressed up because he wants to look his best for *our* wedding.

A photographer is walking along the edge of the lawn with a big telephoto lens, but for once, I'm glad to see them. They signed many pages of paperwork promising to photograph our special day and ensure it's for our eyes only, to be shared with friends in the privacy of our home, not with strangers, splashed across magazines.

I take a deep breath as I come closer, exhaling slowly through my lips. This is it, my wedding day. And I'm walking towards my dream of a husband. How did I get so lucky?

I tap Everett's shoulder and he slowly turns around.

In a classic first-look-moment, he tears up. He takes my hands in his, his dark brown eyes taking in every detail of my hair, my face, my dress, my presence.

"You're so beautiful," he whispers. "You are so beautiful."

"My handsome guy," I reply, giving him a quick kiss because I can and because it's better than any possible combination of words. I use my thumb to wipe my lipstick off his mouth and he smiles.

"Can I go first?" he asks, pulling a piece of paper out of his pocket. His hands are shaking as he unfolds it. He looks to me and I nod for him to go ahead.

"Laina Annalisa Freya Milenna, you are the love of my life

and there is no one on this earth better suited for me than you. You are so out of my league, I shouldn't have had a shot, but the fact that you love me and want to be with me is motivation for me to be the best man I could ever be. You are the calm in my anxious world. You as my wife is an indescribable gift and I am the luckiest man alive. I have always been your protector and that will never change. I promise to put you first, no matter what, and prefer you in all things, as long as we both shall live."

Everett folds his paper and immediately passes his pocket square to me. I have to laugh at the two of us, teary messes just so desperately in love with each other that our emotions never stop overflowing.

I clutch the satin square in my hand as I pull my little rectangle of notebook paper out of my pocket. I didn't expect my voice to shake as much as it does, but I hope he knows it's from sheer gratitude and humility.

"Everett, my rock and my protector, time has only grown my appreciation, respect, admiration, and love for you. To have you as my husband is the greatest honor of my life. You are my soulmate, and there is nothing more worthwhile for me than to be your life partner. I consider it a privilege that I get to be the one to lift you up, to encourage you, and to constantly remind you that you are my favorite person, my treasured friend, and you are my family. I promise to love you with devotion, faithfulness, and joy. Everett, I am yours and you are mine, forever."

I tuck away my paper and the handkerchief and we take each other's hands. There's a moment where we look into each other's eyes, letting our words, our promises to each other sink in. A marriage bond is invisibly woven between us, threading through our hearts and souls, pulling us ever together.

Everett runs his thumb over my hand and I'm reminded of one more thing we have to do.

"Our rings," I say. I'm first to find his new ring in my pocket and I'm so excited my hands are shaking. It's squared-off silver with beveled edges and a matte ribbon in the middle. I bought it a month after he left for Poland. I saw it in the window of an uptown jewelry store and immediately thought, "Everett."

I pull it out and take his left hand in mine, the hand that could have been gone or been limply hanging by his side, but is healthy and whole. I slide his ring on and he marvels at it, flexing his hand, then making a fist.

"You can keep the other one around your neck forever," I say.

"Thank you," he says with a grin. "I love it."

It looks so good on him, I might say forget my ring altogether, let's get to the kissing part. But he's already pulling something out of his pocket, then hiding it in his fist, sheepishly grinning.

"I got you exactly what you asked for. For the record, I wanted to buy you something a lot more expensive, but this is what you wanted and I want you to be happy."

I laugh as he takes off my engagement ring, slips on the plain gold band I requested, then adds the engagement ring back. My first wedding ring adorns my right hand and I love that I have something from him on both hands.

I look up at him with a smile so wide my cheeks ache.

"Thank you, Ev."

"You're welcome," he says, but his eyes are already looking

at my lips and there's no reason not to move to the end of our little wedding.

"You can now kiss your bride," I whisper to him.

He sweeps me up in his arms, picking me up off my feet and spinning me around, while somehow managing to give me the most heart-melting, soul-splitting kiss of my life.

"I'm so going to sleep with you tonight," Everett says in a heated whisper, mid-kiss.

Trust me, I'm the happiest woman alive.

THE BLACK SWAN PROTECTION NOVELLAS

All standalone, closed door romance novellas that can be read in any order.

Stay Close by Keira Dominguez

Trust Me by Hope Snyder

Shield Her by JD Rogers

Last Minute by Ashley Funk

ACKNOWLEDGMENTS

I came up with the idea for Laina and Everett when I was on my certificate course at Cambridge in 2019. I submitted this first chapter as my novel-writing-term final, and got my lowest grade of the entire course. My tutor was not a fan. But the handsome bodyguard and the brave CEO he's charged to protect never left my imagination. I'm so grateful this story finally came to life.

Anna, Charlotte, Erin, Kate, I literally could not have written this book without you. I love you and miss you. Thank you for keeping up our weekly Zoom calls and for every bit of feedback and encouragement you've contributed in the midst of your own busy lives. Pondlife Forever, friends.

Keira, thanks for taking a chance on a fun idea from an unpublished writer last August. From the moment we agreed to give this series the green light, it's been terrifying and incredible. Thank you for your feedback, guidance, communication, and friendship. I am ever so grateful for you.

Ashley, I seriously can't thank you enough for all your work on the cover design, the graphics, the formatting leadership, and so much more. Thank you for ripping into my story with constructive feedback. You absolutely helped take this story to the next level, thanks to voice messages. Thank you!

JD, thank you for jumping on board this crazy train. We couldn't have done this without you. You're one relentless writing warrior and I love talking plot with you. Thank you for bringing your bodyguard magic to the team. You rock.

Rachel and MaryAnn at Ascension Edits, thank you so much for your detailed feedback, editing skills, and enthusiasm for this story. I loved working with both of you!

To all my amazing friends who have cheered me on in my writing journey—thank you, thank you, thank you. You've kept this Navy wife/mom/writer going.

Maddie, I'll never forget the sleepover we had at your house in middle school. You gave me a notebook and a pencil and said, "Let's write some stories." That was the start of me learning to write for joy, unlocking this essential part of myself. Thank you, friend.

To my parents, siblings, and extended family, you are all amazing, incredible people and I'm so grateful for your support and love. Marie, thank you for reading early, rough versions of this story and telling your friends I'm writing a book that they should read. What a compliment.

Kids, thank you for all the hugs and for telling me I'm really good at writing, even though only one of you can read. You're the best, I'm so glad that we get to be a family.

Jake, love of my life, thank you for always being in my corner, for taking leave so I could do solo writing retreats, for cooking me food, for telling people that your wife is a writer. I can only do this because of your love and encouragement. And thanks for the "Indie Author" category in our budget. I love you so much.

Lord, thank you for sustaining me throughout this project, for refreshing my imagination, and for the many loving gifts You've given me throughout my creative journey. All praise and glory to You.

ABOUT THE AUTHOR

Hope Snyder writes love stories full of courage and kissing, always with a happily ever after. She's a Navy wife, a mother of three, an avid reader, and a proud California girl. She has a Certificate in Creative Writing from the University of Cambridge Institute for Continuing Education and has lived all over the world. Constantly on the move due to Navy life, she's most at home when she's working on her next romance novel.

ALSO BY HOPE SNYDER
Care for this Love: A Sweet Navy Romance
Love's Racing Line: A Closed Door Formula One Romance

Connect with Hope at <u>hopesnyderwriter.com</u> where you can sign up for her newsletter for monthly updates!

 instagram.com/hopesnyder_writer